CORVUS AND ME

Copyright © Joëlle Hübner McLean, 2012. All rights reserved. No part of this book may be reproduced or transmitted in any form or by any means, electronic or mechanical, including photocopying, recording, or by any information storage and retrieval system, without permission in writing from the publisher.

Bedside Books
An imprint of American Book Publishing
5442 So. 900 East, #146
Salt Lake City, UT 84117-7204
www.american-book.com
Printed in the United States of America on acid-free paper.

Corvus and Me

Designed by Peter Healy, design@american-book.com

Publisher's Note: This is a work of fiction. Names, characters, places, and incidents either are the product of the author's imagination, or are used fictitiously, and any resemblance to actual persons, living or dead, events, or locales is entirely coincidental.

ISBN-13: 978-1-58982-665-6

ISBN-10: 1-58982-665-5

Hübner-McLean, Joëlle; Corvus and Me

Special Sales

These books are available at special discounts for bulk purchases. Special editions, including personalized covers, excerpts of existing books, and corporate imprints, can be created in large quantities for special needs. For more information e-mail info@american-book.com.

Corvus and Me
Joëlle Hübner-McLean

Joëlle Hübner-McLean
xoxo

This is for my Maman, Papa, and younger sister.

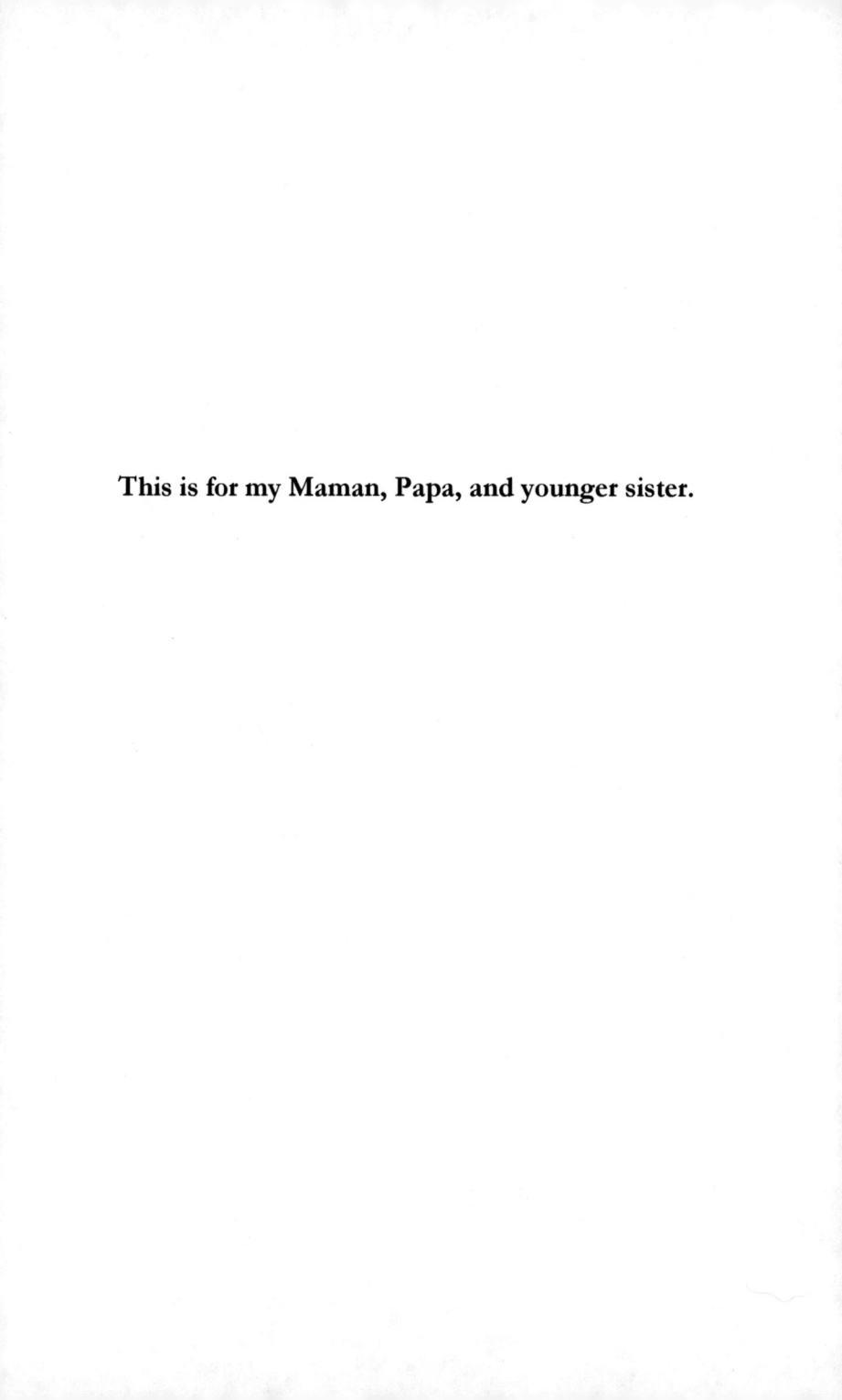

1

Only a few woodland birds remain in their breeding territory year round, and their strength lies in the ability to adapt to the harsh winters in Canada.

Soaring in the crisp, blue sky, Corvus, the crow, has been there for Janine upon request. After all, Janine is by nature an adventurer who feels compelled to investigate the world around her, just like the crow.

She was visiting her favorite place, about a mile-and-a-half away from civilization into the woods, but she was unclear as to why she was lying there in the snow, all alone and not a bird or animal in sight. Janine checked her body for injuries but found none. The big question now was whether or not Janine was imagining the whole thing or if it was real. And, more importantly, why was she not feeling the cold or dampness from the snow? Janine also wondered where her sister had gotten to. Maybe she has given up on complaining about being cold and is amusing herself somewhere in the small woods, or perhaps she was headed home. But why is it so still?

Noticing that the darkness was nearing and it was a long trek towards home, Janine began to worry and called out, but heard no sound or answer. Trying again to communicate vocally, she was still unsuccessful. As Janine stood up and began brushing the snow from her blue snowsuit, she realized that a serious situation had suddenly landed in her lap. She was all alone. She began to look for her sister in the woods but was unsuccessful. At that point the disappearance of her sister began to worry her. Where could she be? It was unlike her to leave Janine unaccompanied; how would her parents react to such a dilemma? Janine knew very well that her parents would be concerned, and would not tolerate her being out for so long. Janine also knew that her parents were overprotective and may prevent her from going out for a long time.

She would be very unhappy if that happened.

In a sense, she was aware of their feelings of being that way only because they were never exposed to civilization, living at a distance from one another, and living in a strange country is even more frightening. Her parents used to live in two large populated cities---Paris, France and West Berlin, Germany---where accessibility was available close at hand, before they immigrated to Canada. She was sure that her parents would miss her terribly and had visions of her mother calling her name with a "whooo" sound to get her attention.

It was time to get her thoughts together, but how was she going to explain the loss of her sister? Janine needed to make noise, lots of noise, in order to attract her sister's attention. So, Janine tried to call again, but no sound was heard. What was wrong with her voice? She tried again and again, but still no sound was coming out of her mouth. It was then she decided to look for her sister more closely since she wore a pink snowsuit with a cream-colored scarf. Janine was sure she could spot the snowsuit in an instant, but after inspecting all the places around her, there was still no result. It was time to return home in hope that her sister did the same thing. It was then that tears began to stream down her face, as she began to walk slowly through the small woods, with daylight beginning to fade away.

Janine began to believe that she had reached her fate. But she refused to go without a fight. The only thing to do now was to head towards home and hope that her sister returned safely. Even though Janine made her decision, she still had a breaking point and began to cry while she trudged through the small woods. Time was running out since the darkness was nearing, and she knew she would not reach home before nightfall.

2

"Hello, little girl," said Right Whisper, with a soft voice. "Are you all right?"

"What? Who said that?" asked Janine as she tripped and fell, looking around to see who was spying on her.

"It is I, Right Whisper."

"Show yourself," Janine shouted, as she picked up a small branch to defend herself. "Who are you? Show yourself before I…"

"Before you try to hurt me with that thing," laughed Right Whisper. "Think again. It is impossible to destroy me unless you have powerful force or a Swede saw! Now put that twig down before you hurt yourself."

Janine perused her surroundings, baffled as to who was speaking to her with such a kind but authoritative voice.

"I am warning you, stop hiding and show yourself, unless you are afraid that I might hurt you," Janine said.

"Feisty little runt," murmured Right Whisper. With a softer tone, Right Whisper then said, "Again, tiny one, I am not afraid of you and if you must see me, turn your head to the right and walk towards the sound of my voice."

"Which way?" asked Janine.

"Over here. Where the sound is coming from, silly." Right Whisper chuckled. "Keep coming, you are getting warmer."

"Am I there yet, because I am really having problems seeing you?" Janine cautiously inquired.

"You are almost in front of me."

"Where? I do not see you."

"One more step to the right and bravo! You made it. You have found the voice of mystery and no one got hurt," said Right Whisper.

"Okay, this is a joke, right?"

"How did you know my name was Right?"

By this time Janine was confused, thinking that someone else was there but playing a joke on her.

"You know this is not funny. I need to go home right away and I can't see you. Please show yourself. I have no time for playing games and I feel silly talking to a tree! I would be very embarrassed if someone would show up and find me talking to a tree. Can you imagine what my family would say? I'll tell you, they would laugh at me." Janine was rambling in her frustration.

"I do not know a 'Right', and you are certainly confusing me since I am still looking for you or it or whatever you are. I do not know how long I have been here in the woods and I am supposed to return home, and now I am speaking to a tree! How ridiculous is that? Can you imagine what my parents or school friends might say if they caught me talking to a tree? They would laugh at me and probably send me to a loony bin for the rest of my life."

"You are too much, missy. You get yourself in a tizzy. What a sense of humor you have. You are right though; you are talking right at me. Welcome, little one, to the talking tree."

Janine was stunned. She observed both sides of the tree, walked around it twice, and found no clue where the person with the ventriloquist voice was hiding.

"Right, I give up." Janine threw her stick away. "I will wait until you wish to communicate with me face to face."

"Listen, little one, let me introduce myself again. My name is Right Whisper."

"Right what?"

"Right Whisper, at your service. Also known as Acer saccharum."

"Acer sacc…?"

"Acer saccharum, a Latin word for sugar maple, which we are generally called in this part of the woods; a very popular tree. One day you will learn about different trees from this part of the country in your science classes, but right now you are talking to a maple tree, Canada's national tree, also known as Acer saccharum. When you learn science one day you will learn that around the Great Lakes to the St. Lawrence region is known as a transition forest. I might add that this forest is in a broad transitional zone, mixed in with a mosaic of northern needle-leaved trees and southern broad-leaved deciduous trees as far as they can adapt to the climate at hand. But, you can call me Right Whisper."

For an instant Janine did not know what to make of all of this. Maybe this was all a hoax. She was taught at home to not expect things right away and be patient. She was still not quite convinced that she was just talking to a tree. She realized that something or someone hit her on the back of her head, which possibly could have given her a concussion. So she decided to remain calm and polite because the ventriloquist person, whoever it may be, could be dangerous. And when the right time came, she would outsmart the treacherous individual, face to face. In the meantime, while remaining charming and well mannered, Janine, too, introduced herself.

"Since you were kind enough to introduce yourself, I am called Janine. How do you do?" she said as she accidentally extended her hand, but realized almost instantaneously that she was speaking to a deciduous.

"Well it is a pleasure to meet you finally, Janine. I have waited a long time for this moment, for your arrival, and the right season I might add," said Right Whisper. "You don't have to shake hands with me, since I have no arms."

Retrieving her hand quickly, Janine gracefully apologized for her ignorance. Observing the situation at hand, she recognized that the voice was quite soothing and kind. Hoping that no one was watching her, Janine decided to speak to the tree with caution.

"If you don't mind me asking, where are your arms and legs?" she asked, thinking her plan would work to weed out the perpetrator. While looking around her with great precision, she thought she saw something out of the corner of her eye, but was unable to identify what it was as Right Whisper answered.

"When there is a heavy snowfall, my appearance grows on the walls of the crevice of the trees to expose my identity. Being an old tree, the outermost layers of this bark are split into corky ridges, which the snow can cling to. Therefore, your imagination perceives itself into a form of existence of a human face with no arms or legs at times."

With disbelief and curiosity, Janine found no clue at the moment that no one of existence was present, but only the two of them among the solitude of the forest who were talking to each other. Or were they?

3

"Well, do you believe me now, Janine?" asked Right Whisper. "Will you now position yourself so that we can speak face to face?"

Janine slowly moved her body to the right of the tree to view Right Whisper with proper respect when being spoken to.

"Ah!" screamed Janine. "I now see your eyes and your mouth! I can see them moving!"

"That is much better. I don't have to strain my eyes looking for you anymore. As I was telling you before, I do not have arms and legs, just a face outlined due to how the snow blows onto the tree, and you, my friend, are the only human on earth that can speak to me like this at the moment. Yes, other humans visualize faces and bodies and so on too, but they lack the imagination and sensitivity to the forest's needs. That is where they fail."

With a questionable look Janine asked, "How is that possible? Every time I wander into the woods I converse to myself."

"Exactly, and now it is our turn to reciprocate our feelings to you and lead you on a journey of make-believe, where you can now communicate with anyone you wish to speak to in this world or not, except..."

"Except?" She was determined to know whom she was not able to speak to. "Please tell me!"

"Well, you had to open your big mouth again, didn't you, lassie?" shouted Heartwood as Janine let out a scream and backed away from the trees as soon as she heard Heartwood bellow in a harsh Scottish accent. "Did you think I was going to hurt you now? Come, come now, you mustn't be afraid, young lass. Heartwood is the name. I am not here to hurt you, but my dear friend" (as his bushy brown eyebrows pointed towards Right Whisper) "can't seem to keep her big mouth shut and be a wee bit more subtle! I am sorry about this whole business. I apologize for my friend's unethical way of producing a desperate need for help."

He then turned his attention to Right Whisper. "Give the poor girl a break. Seemingly, you have decided to place her on a mission before she could grasp the fact that she is talking to two trees!"

Heartwood waved his branches to and fro as he stood tall, opposite to Right Whisper. "How do you know we can even trust her in the few short minutes you spoke to her. You have done it this time, Whisper. You put your big root into your big mouth and you expect this girl to respond to our request just like that? You are such a trusting tree, but you are about to put a burden on this poor young lassie."

"Her name is..." as Right Whisper ignored her buddy, only to be interrupted again by Heartwood.

"Snow Sleeper. She is the queen of the winter season and right now, we, meaning the forest, are quite concerned with what will be happening with all the animals and birds since the winter season is quite harsh at the moment. Too many days have passed without a break from continuous freezing rain and snow. Yes, they are well protected under the trees for now, but food is scarce and the animals and birds will starve or freeze to death if this does not stop soon. There are many who have already fallen victim and we do not have the capability to find Snow Sleeper anywhere. So…"

"So, we're wondering if you would not mind helping us," Right Whisper interrupted.

"Don't most birds fly south and animals hibernate?" asked Janine.

"Yes!" both Right Whisper and Heartwood answered.

"So, what makes this winter different from all the other winters we've had in the past?"

"Well, I have not seen any signs of the queen to warn the birds and animals and prepare them for the hard times to come. Her regular rounds have been long overdue since the last winter and the forest is quite concerned about her negligence and whereabouts."

"What makes you think that I could find the…the…"

"Snow Sleeper," Heartwood and Right Whisper answered simultaneously.

"Right. Snow Sleeper, and save all the precious birds and animals. That seems impossible! Besides, being by myself with no help makes it even harder to do. I would not know where to begin."

"You are right, but before it is too late, you need… You love animals and birds, don't you?" asked Right Whisper.

"Yes."

"Well, then I was right in picking you as the appointed candidate to locate where Snow Sleeper is residing and help us save our kingdom."

"What if I refuse this mission?"

"I knew it. Just another lassie full of ideas, but lacking the guts!" remarked Heartwood.

"Quiet, Heartwood, we do not want to discourage Janine at this moment."

"Do you want to return home?" asked Right Whisper.

"I still can and you cannot stop me," Janine stated. "You are only a tree."

"You are absolutely correct, but…"

"But, nothing. I have arms. I have legs and I can walk away from here whenever I please and you, or should I say *both of you*, cannot stop me."

"They will not see you as who you really are, Janine," said Right Whisper.

Looking confused and startled, Janine stopped, turned around and walked slowly towards the talking deciduous.

"What did you say?"

"They will not see you!"

"*They*, meaning my parents and sister, will not see me? Is that what you mean by that?"

"Grab that piece of ice close by you and hold it in front of me."

Reluctantly, Janine followed the orders, and searched for small potholes in the ground covered with ice near the crevices of dead trees, and with some difficulty was able to crack the ice with the heal of her boot; she then brought a jagged small piece of ice with some frozen grass attached to it to the tree. Right Whisper disapproved of the size of the ice, so Janine tried two more times until Right Whisper was satisfied with the size of the frozen slab.

"This will do. Now, place the piece of ice on my trunk and observe closely."

With anticipation Right Whisper directed Janine on how to keep the piece of ice steady, packing it with snow on the sides to keep the ice from falling. All of a sudden, the ice began to form into an elaborate mirror. Janine was mesmerized by the magical moment. Not knowing what to do next, her eyes were glued onto the mirror, absorbing breathlessly the contents that appeared. She observed a time zone she was quite familiar with. Watching curiously, she saw herself dancing, singing, making up songs, and being extremely energetic.

The setting in the reflection was a sunny afternoon when Janine's sister, Elisabeth, and she completed their weekend chores and decided to take their sleigh with them. They took turns pulling one another as they neared the big hill by the forest. To their surprise, not only did they anticipate a long journey down the snowy hill, but gasped at the sight of the icy incline. Never had they seen such a sight. They noticed a wired fence below, and because the hill was part of the farmer's property, the cows were prevented from escaping the land by the fence. Every winter the hill is covered with ice and snow, and sure footing is important to prevent one from falling down the hill, but no one has had the opportunity to try it out to go sleighing or tobogganing. The challenge is how fast they will go before they hit the fence.

Janine and her sister decided to try it out at least once.

Being the oldest of the siblings, Janine positioned the sleigh where it would give them the most distance from the top of the hill, and balanced it so that her sister could sit comfortably. Once situated at the front of the sleigh, and using her feet to stabilize it, her sister sat easily, wrapped her arms around Janine's waist, and placed her feet underneath Janine's thighs. Janine used her body to move the sleigh so that it would slide down the hill.

With great speed, the sled flew down the hill, hitting every bump through its passage, and causing their seats to hurt whenever they landed on the hard planks of the sled. Steering the sleigh while it was racing downhill took some skill in order to prevent the two of them from falling off.

Janine's sister still ended up falling off near the end of the ride at the foot of the hill while Janine held on, crossing the field below into the wired fence and landing on the frozen marsh. Suddenly, Janine came to a dead stop.

To Janine's relief, she and her sister were not harmed, but they soon realized that they had a long, slippery walk back to the top. It was then Janine's sister decided to decline the second jaunt of going down the big icy hill. Janine, on the other hand, wanted to try racing the sleigh down the treacherous hill once again to see how far the sled might go with only one person on it. The climb would not be easy since the icy hill had few clumps of grass to use as stability while pulling the sleigh; she was not going to let that discourage her from reaching the top.

With her heart pumping fast, Janine observed carefully, looking for different areas of the terrain where she could steer the sleigh with less bumps and more ice. She experienced the rush the first time and wanted to have it last longer the second time.

She was right. The sleigh did go far and it was fun. Janine's sister watched her go down the hill again and yelled out that she wanted to head for home as soon as possible because she was dreadfully cold. As Janine climbed up the icy hill with her sleigh once again, she thought to herself that she was not ready to return home just yet. Once she reached the bottom of the hill, she ignored her sister's plea, and decided to go through the small forest because it was a longer way back towards her home.

Even though the sun was shining, it was still very cold and the level of the snow was quite deep. In most cases it would come up to a child's waistline at nine years old, which was a task for a youngster to trek through.

Janine continued to play in the small forest and convinced Elisabeth to stay for a while, but it was not long before her sister complained again about being cold and wanting to return home. As usual, Janine refused to go, even though her sister persisted to go home on her own, crying with pain. Janine generally followed her sister only to guard her from falling or to keep her warm from the cold winds, but this time Janine decided to spend a little more time exploring her environment and not tag along with her sister.

If it were not because of her selfishness, she would have been home comfortable and cozy, with no worries of getting into trouble from her parents for being late. At this point, Janine would surely be punished for her selfishness.

It was then that the mirror showed a visual impression of her fall: Janine lost her footing on an icy patch and fell backwards onto the sleigh striking the back of her head onto a felled tree. Not knowing what to do, Janine's younger sister swiftly went over to examine Janine, calling out her name. When Janine did not respond, her sister fled the scene and proceeded to dash towards home, crying all the way.

It was then when the mirror went blank.

Corvus & Me

4

"Oaf! That took a lot of energy out of me," said Right Whisper.

"Where is the rest of it?"

"What do you mean the rest of it?" said Right Whisper softly.

"The rest of what happened!"

"There is no more," said Right Whisper.

"Do you mean that I do not exist in the real world?'

"Well, yes and no," Right Whisper said with some hesitation.

Mystified by answer, Janine questioned Right Whisper again.

"You are scaring me; it's either I exist or I don't exist! I can feel the cold air, and I can see my hand in front of face, but I'm still talking to a tree. What's going on?"

Trying to rationalize what had just happened, Janine walked away from Right Whisper and began to converse with herself in order to make sense of all of this.

"Okay, now, Janine, calm down and rationalize what is happening to you," she told herself as she paced back and forth.

"Will you listen to me, Janine!" exclaimed Right Whisper. "Yes, at the moment your soul still exists, but your body doesn't. Your spirit, or soul, is speaking to me right now and if you remember that you hit your head, your body still remains in tack. You have always spoken to us from your heart and now it is more centralized."

"What? Did someone call me? Who needs me? I heard my name," snorted Heartwood.

"No, Heartwood. I am still speaking to Janine. Have you been snoozing again while we are in the middle of an important crisis?"

Heartwood remained silent.

"As I was saying, Janine, your inside voice speaks the truth, but unfortunately you never received a response. Well, this is your opportunity now to communicate to us personally."

"What do you mean by personally?" Janine asked as she approached Right Whisper.

"Too many times your little voice inside seems to work a mile a minute and we cannot catch up with the first thought you think about in order for us to help you," said Right Whisper.

"What she means," snorted Heartwood, " is that when you are on your own about to do something important, or a tragic occurrence has developed, you tend to think or analyze the situation using your little voice inside to make a decision for yourself as to how to solve the crisis. Most of the time your instincts are right. In other words, you are not real in the human world, but you are in ours."

"So, you mean that my little voice is now outside my body instead of inside and my thoughts are actually speaking to you?" asked Janine.

"Yes, that is exactly what is happening. Which is a good thing because we desperately need your help now that we can speak to you face to face," Right Whisper said softly.

"Am I dead?"

"No, just unconscious."

"For how long?"

With some hesitation, Right Whisper spoke compassionately to the child. "That all depends on you."

Facing Right Whisper, Janine looked sincere and was not sure what to say to alleviate the fear of the unknown.

"Look, Janine, I realize this is all new to you at the moment and extremely difficult to grasp, but you will surely get use to it sooner or later. We are all counting on you to find Snow Sleeper."

"You keep saying *we*. Who are *we*?"

"Hmmm, 'scuse me, Janine," Heartwood said while clearing his throat.

"You would be surprised to hear that there are quite a few of us that are willing to help you find the queen of the winter season! Yet, there may be a wee small chance that you may not find her due to your lack of powers."

"I have powers?"

"Of course humans have powers. That is, if Faeran, the phantom of fear or anxiety, does not get in the way first."

"The phantom of fear? Anxiety? What is that, and who is Faeran? You guys are confusing me!"

"It is not just who, but what it represents!" explained Right Whisper. "When you and your sister slid down the icy hill, did you feel scared at all?"

"A little," declared Janine.

"Which was worse: sliding down the icy hill or taking a mathematical test that you hate?

"A mathematical test."

"Why?"

"Because I don't like mathematics. Particularly the word problems," Janine admitted.

"What happens to you when you know you have to write a mathematics test?" Right Whisper asked.

"Well," (Janine looked down at her feet) "my stomach gets sick, and I feel like I am going to throw up."

"The pain that you feel in your stomach is caused from fear. You are too emotional when you feel threatened or in danger and then you think of negative things. This causes you to be powerless and anxious. That is why you get so sick in your stomach my little one."

"Okay..."

"Personal fear happens to everyone, Janine," Right Whisper explained sympathetically.

"But, there is more to it than that!" cried Janine.

"Now look what you have done!" said Heartwood. "We have meant no harm, Janine, but we do need your help, and what Right Whisper is trying to say is that you may be faced with unexpected surprises."

Janine tried to compose herself while she listened to Heartwood. "What kind of surprises, and who, or what, is Faeran?"

"Faeran is the leader of all fears, and whenever you feel powerless or threatened, he sends the others to ensure that you lose. The others may not allow you to find Snow Sleeper."

"But what about the birds and animals who are dying from starvation? What about them? Don't they count?"

"You are absolutely right, Janine," stated Heartwood. "But there are the *others* who may not feel the same way. So I have heard," answered Heartwood firmly.

"What are you talking about? Are you dense?" declared Right Whisper.

"Well!" Heartwood said. "You don't have to be rude about it."

"Now, look who opened his big mouth this time!" said Right Whisper. "I am so sorry, Janine, but since Heartwood mentioned Faeran's reinforcement, I will not lie to you. The *others* do exist."

"It is funny you should mention these *others*, because I thought I saw something move a few minutes ago. Like a shadow or something," explained Janine.

"Did you now?" inquired Right Whisper. "It is time, Heartwood, for her to move on to find Snow Sleeper without a moment to lose."

"Yes, yes, it is time. You are absolutely right, Right Whisper. She should get ready for the journey and receive protection against Faeran," said Heartwood.

"If you wish to return home, Janine, you must help us first and I will guide your journey as much as I can," explained Right Whisper.

"How will I do that, Right Whisper?" she asked.

"Well, there are two things you need to do initially. See that lonely old tree behind me a few feet away?"

"The one that stands tall with branches few and far between?" asked Janine, feeling rather sad for the old tree standing alone from all the other trees.

"Yes, that is the one. Her name is J. Regia and she will direct you to the old lady who takes care of the tree by cleaning up all of its fallen walnuts. You need protection from the outside forces. From Faeran."

"What is the second thing I need to do before I leave?"

"The second thing you need to do is to break off the piece of ice from my chest and take it with you if you require me in a time of need."

Trying not to hurt Right Whisper, or so she assumed, she gently began to break some pieces of the ice around the edges until she was satisfied it was small enough to put in her snowsuit

"That's right, keep pulling until it is free and place it close to your heart."

"Won't it melt inside my winter coat?"

"No, it will not, because once it is close to your heart, nature's magic will keep it from melting. Now hurry along and meet with J. Regia so that the journey may begin."

"By the way," exclaimed Janine, "I have another question to ask you, Right Whisper. Where did you get your name from?"

"Well, to make a long story short, when you first glanced at me last winter, I was about twenty feet away from you on your right side. And instead of being called, Acer saccharum, I adopted the name Right Whisper. Here they call me, 'Whisper,' for short because I carry such a soft voice."

"Well, what about Heartwood?"

"It is a wee bit difficult to explain to a nine-year-old, but it is all part of the sapwood production of a hardwood deciduous tree. When you take science in school your teachers will be able to help you understand the process of a growing hardwood tree. That is as much as I will tell you because you have to skedaddle," grunted Heartwood.

"That is pretty lame, Heartwood. But you are right. You need to move along, Janine," said Right Whisper.

Janine finally released the mirror and placed it gently inside her snowsuit. While saying goodbye to Heartwood, she felt that one day she would be able to see him again.

"Goodbye, Heartwood. It was nice meeting you!"

Her next stop was J. Regia.

5

As Janine carefully approached the old tree, she went over in her mind what she was going to say to it. As she summoned the tree's name several times, she decided to wait until J. Regia spoke. It felt like an eternity had passed before J. Regia finally responded.

"How do you know my name and why are you here to bother me?"

"I...I apologize for waking you up, J. Regia, but I need your help locating the old lady that gathers your walnuts in the fall."

"What is your purpose to find the old lady, if you do not mind me asking?"

"Well, I am on a mission to find the snow queen."

"Nonsense!" bellowed the old tree. "No one can find the snow queen or has been able to find any trace of her whereabouts. What makes you think you can?"

"I don't know, but Right Whisper and Heartwood seem to have trust in me and think that I am able to help them find her. Using the right directions and some guidance, I hope to find her so that I may return home safe and as soon as possible."

The old tree observed the little girl carefully and realized how sincere she was when she spoke. Conversing in a much tender tone the old tree said, "Little girl, what is your name?"

"Janine."

"A very pretty name. I will direct you to where the old woman lives, provided you keep it a secret. Do you understand me?"

"Yes, yes, I do. Thank you," said Janine with hesitation, realizing how tough the old tree was, even though she was ancient.

"Listen carefully, Janine. Before I give you the instructions as to where to find the old lady, you must do a good deed for me in order to continue. It is like a test."

"What do I have to do?" questioned Janine anxiously.

"Well, it might be difficult, but I do hope you will give it a try before you bail out without understanding it first."

"Is it going to be difficult, because sometimes my mind goes blank when I am nervous?" Janine asked as she tried to calm her emotions.

Looking at Janine with disapproval, J. Regia said, "Do you always question other's integrity when someone is giving you advice? Did your parents not teach you any manners?"

"What does integrity mean?"

"Integrity? Well, it means honesty. Do you not trust my truthfulness when I tell you something that is important?"

Janine's eyes started to swell up with tears. "Well, I am honest too, and I never seem to get it with tests."

There was a short period of silence before J. Regia responded. "You have obviously been there before, so I did not mean to upset you since you are the chosen one and I am a little rusty and rough around the edges with my manners to children, Janine. It has been a while since I have spoken to a youngster and I suppose I need a lesson or two as to how to communicate effectively without hurting anyone's feelings. I do apologize. Please give me another chance to explain what needs to be done here."

Janine wiped her eyes with the cold sleeve of her snowsuit and looked up with a sad face. She hoped that she could complete her task successfully. Swallowing hard, she spoke softly. "I will do my best. That is all I can promise you, J. Regia."

"Good! Now, listen carefully. You must walk towards that small bush on your left and you must find Corvus Brachyrhynchos as soon as possible and bring him here."

"Corvus Brach...?"

"Corvus Brachy means "short" and rynochos means "bill." He is a large black crow who has a slight sight problem."

"Why?"

"Because it is important that he is brought back to me. I need to see him immediately. Can you do that for me? Here on my left? In these bushes?" Janine looked in the instructed direction.

"Yes, keep looking. He is in there somewhere. I heard him crash into the bushes earlier and he hasn't come back to me, yet."

Janine walked into the bushes capped with snow as directed and looked high and low, but was unable to see anything until she heard a moan not far from a trunk of a small maple tree. As she approached, she noticed a black blob of something close to the edge of the tree, stretched out upside down, whining like a small child. As she got closer, she saw that it was a bird. She gently pulled this fairly large, black body out the snow bank and noticed that it was a crow. It was about two feet tall.

She had always wanted to befriend a crow because of its iridescent violet, glossy body and its intelligence. Having had the experience at home of saving birds and animals, she recognized that there was still hope for this beautiful crow to survive. Quickly, she picked up the bird and ran towards the old tree, amused by her finding. She realized that the black crow was still alive, and she was happy with the thought that she was able to save its life. With careful footing and a watchful eye as to where she was going, she kept hoping the bird would not die in her hands as she approached the old tree.

"What do you want me to do with it? I did hear it moaning earlier," she said as she stood there holding it very gently.

"I would like you to place the bird right side up, next to me, and rest it on its stomach without hurting its feet, and check to see if it's bleeding anywhere."

Being very careful in handling the fragile bird, Janine lightly positioned the crow on its stomach and softly laid its head to one side. She noticed that the bird's eyes were half-opened. In her mind, she thought this crow was unconscious and badly hurt, and that it may eventually die if not cared for properly. Janine remembered when a bird or animal was injured at home; it was important to make them comfortable and warm with available water nearby. If they had been seriously hurt, then they needed to be taken to the veterinary immediately, but if they had a slight injury, then they needed rest until recovered.

Janine examined the bird and felt the chest cavity moving ever so slightly. It was then she told J. Regia that the crow was still alive.

"Good. Now it is a matter of waiting until Corvus wakes up, but until then, you must find some flat, dead grass by the marsh to keep him warm."

"Do you mean that I have to go all the way to the bottom of the icy hill *again* and into the marsh?"

"Of course you need to go down to the marsh. Do you want to pass the test or not?"

"Of course I want to pass, but why don't I save some time by using my scarf or my hat to keep the crow warm?"

"No! It's grass or nothing. Do you want his death to be on your conscience?"

"It will take me a while to do this. Are you sure it is going to work?"

J. Regia's expression changed when two brown eyes appeared in the trunk and the two center crevices from its bark joined one another into a horizontal smile and answered, "Quite sure."

The thought of sliding down the icy hill was paramount, but climbing up would be a challenge. And getting back as soon as possible in order to save the crow life was Janine's main concern.

Looking forward to once again gliding downhill with the use of her wooden sleigh, Janine got ready on top of the summit. Positioning and balancing her sled on a crevice, she sat on the sleigh ever so gently. Grabbing the rope that controlled the steering on one hand and arranging her scarf around her face with the other hand, Janine placed her feet on the footrest in front of the sleigh. Giving herself a little push with her small body, the sleigh suddenly released itself from the crevice and movement began.

Descending quickly on the ice, over the bumps wrestling against the unchartered hill, Janine maneuvered the sled into the correct path, through the wired fence, and into the marsh. Once the skis hit the grass, the sled stopped dead and Janine almost lost her stability, but she positioned her feet on the ground in time to maintain her composure.

Boosting herself up from the sleigh, Janine looked for an abundant turf of grass, suitable for the lame crow to be at ease and hopefully retrieve consciousness from its traumatic accident.

Using her judgment as to the amount of grass to gather for the crow, Janine began her trek back up the icy hill.

Losing her grip several times while climbing the hill, she positioned her feet on the areas where her body could feel more secure while she climbed. Janine kept an eye on the grass while she pulled the sleigh and finally reached her destination, letting go of the rope. She grabbed the grass from the sled and ran to the old tree as planned.

"Quick, shut your eyes, she's coming!" remarked J. Regia to Corvus.

Janine fell on her knees and caught her breath while placing the grass over the injured bird. A few minutes later Janine was startled by the crow's remarkable recovery as it began to sputter and cough.

"Well, it is about time! A bird can freeze out here without moving. I need to stretch my wings and shake this body into shape," said Corvus as he jumped to his feet and began fluffing his feathers and straightening his posture. Then speaking rather quickly, he said, "Whooie. That was quite the thrill. I can't believe I missed that landing. I was like a roller coaster without wheels. Man, after that, I can't remember what happened," the crow said.

"Well, whatever the case, I am here, ain't I? I mean, *aren't* I?" Corvus examined his wings. "Ah! Look at this sh.., I mean look at these wings. Oh man, these wings look like I took a swim in a sewer. Will you look at this? I can't believe I look like a scarecrow. My predecessors would turn over in their graves and say, 'Hey, grease ball, feel a little drafty? Who did your brushing?' "

Janine just stood there dumbfounded and tried to make sense of what was coming out of the crow's mouth. She then decided to interrupt him. "Are you all right? How are you feeling? You sure recovered fast."

"Feeling? It's cold and wet. It doesn't matter which way you look at it. We crows love the heat most of the time, yet where do I end up? Here in the land of icicles. I had plans, big plans, before I turned up here. My friends are migrating to the south and plan on having a good time, but no, not me. It's seeds on frozen bacon fat. Well, little girl, judging by the look on your face, you must think I am selfish, but I'm not. That's the way things are in my world." Corvus cawed.

"Don't pay any attention to him, Janine. He is somewhat upset that he missed the tree and was chosen to serve and protect. But deep down he really, truly cares about his mission to help you find the old lady and the snow queen," explained J. Regia.

"Well, he surely has a funny way of expressing himself," commented Janine.

"He is rough around the edges with his words, but he is a very good soul," answered J. Regia.

"Well, Janine, shall we save the world of animals and birds? The sooner we head off, the sooner I can sink my scrawny legs in the hot sand," said Corvus as he signaled Janine to get a head start. Once she was at a safe distance, he knew that J. Regia had last minute instructions to give him

"Keep an eye on Janine, Corvus, and whatever you do, use excellent judgment in keeping her out of trouble and harm's way," J. Regia pointed out.

"I'll do my best, J.R!"

"Goodbye!" shouted Janine as she began to follow Corvus into the woods.

6

Janine only listened to half of what was going on between Corvus and J. Regia, but still realized that she needed to prepare herself to follow the crow until the task was over. Feeling scared about what was ahead of her, she had confidence in her soul that no matter what would happen, she would do her best to make it right. She wrapped her scarf around her neck, mouth, and nose, and concentrated on following the crow that was flying above her. It was not until the crow was out of sight for a second or two when Right Whisper spoke softly to Janine from inside her coat.

"Watch your step, Janine. If you drop me, all will be lost and we cannot risk the failure of your mission. It was a close call when you went down that hill, so try to arrange me so that I will be secure in your snowsuit."

"Right," said Janine, and followed the instructions by making sure that she positioned the ice mirror so that Right Whisper was safe inside her snowsuit. For a moment, Janine lost sight of Corvus while she arranged the mirror, but finally located him in the sky and kept a close eye on him while she battled the strong winter wind and the deep snow. There were times when she fell flat on her face trying to catch up with the crow, but with determination, she kept up her pace.

While she followed Corvus, Janine had the sudden feeling that she was not alone. At times she would get a glimpse of a shadowy object following her, but through her peripheral vision, she could only see slight movement.

The journey was strenuous. At times her footing would give way to hidden potholes, and other times her boots would get stuck in the snow and cause her to stumble.

The more Janine thought of her mission, the more she felt incompetent. She would ask herself questions about whether or not she would be able to find Snow Sleeper. Janine was getting more and more doubtful with the whole idea of whether she was going to save the snow queen or be a disappointment.

Her breathing was getting more and more shallow due to her asthma attacks, so she knew that she had to rest for a while so that she may continue. As she stopped to control her wheezing, she recognized that she was on unfamiliar grounds and simultaneously happened to spot more shadows pursuing her.

Seconds later, Corus flew over Janine's head and mentioned that they were getting closer to their destination. He suggested to Janine to stop thinking of negative thoughts and concentrate only on their mission. Shocked by his statement, Janine was about to ask how he knew, when he immediately hurried onward, swooping over her head and almost hitting another tree.

They suddenly came to a farmhouse surrounded by a fence and mature trees. As she looked around, she realized it was a familiar cattle farm next to a dirt road about two miles away from her parents' home. She walked up to a nearby fence post and stood there observing the property.

Janine could remember when the cattle would frequently appear in the field across from her house where Uncle Tom, the farm's owner, would sometimes make a special trip to bring them back to the barn. The cows would immediately obey his commands and turn around and head for home. Once in a while the cows would run away, but eventually Uncle Tom would get them back on track.

There it was: a two-storey red brick farmhouse with small white-framed windows; the A-line one-storey wooden barn with a red tin roof and three small windows on each side was behind the farmhouse, which was large enough to accommodate about fifteen to twenty cows.

Janine knew right away where she was because whenever she traveled with her parents on the dirt road, the farmhouse was in sight. Shortly thereafter, Corvus landed on the fence post beside her.

7

"This is Uncle Tom's cattle farm! And his cows and two bulls are somewhere close, but I am not about to find out, just in case they chase me! So, I am not walking any further," exclaimed Janine, realizing that the wind had died down.

"Ya! Is it not grand? Open field means easy prey."

"Don't you generally pick on dead animals on the side of the road or anything that is already dead?"

Corvus shook his head with agreement. "I do, but if it is small and it tempts me, then it's mine."

"Oh! How disgusting," retorted Janine as she walked away from him.

"That is the nature of my being, Janine," answered Corvus.

"Aren't we trespassing on Uncle Tom's land anyway?" asked Janine.

"No, we ain't. I mean, aren't. And besides, you know him, don't you? So what difference does it make? He cannot see you, and why do you have to be so critical of what I do or think? I've got to eat, you know. I've haven't had solid food for weeks."

"Uncle Tom can't see us?" Janine thought of what Right Whisper told her in the beginning.

"No, not unless he has X-ray eyes, or he is dead, and the last time I checked, he wasn't," replied Corvus. "And to answer your question as to whether I know him or not, I don't know him personally. Wait, I think someone is coming this way."

Janine and Corvus crouched down behind the water trough near the barn. Slowly she looked up, over the trough, to see who was coming out of the barn. It was then she recognized Uncle Tom, looking mighty weary, and heading towards the farmhouse. Once Uncle Tom was out of sight, Corvus felt confident to speak to Janine.

"We may not be too late. We must wait for a while or until Uncle Tom goes back to the barn minding the cattle."

"Why?"

"Why? Because it gives us a chance to meet with the old lady; you see, she doesn't come out until…"

"Meet the old lady? Are you telling me that the old lady is…"

"She's dead!" Corvus said. "She is bone-dry dead!"

Janine stared at Corvus with a soft frown on her face and said, "Does she know we are here?"

"Maybe, maybe not."

At this time Janine had doubts of whether she wished to see the old lady or not. Would the old woman really want to?

While Corvus sat beside Janine, he said, "Listen, do not give up now, Janine. The old broad, I mean, this old lady, loves her husband and she never left the farm unless she absolutely had to. I could remember her hunting and skinning rabbits for rabbit stew, milking the cows, the whole shebang. She still hasn't changed: her brown hair, uptight in a bun, a flowery dress with full apron protecting her dress, and she's always wearing rubber boots. Ema hasn't changed a bit. That's her name, you know. So that is why you and me need to go and see her and…"

Janine interrupted Corvus, "Why?"

"Why? Well, I…How can I put it delicately without hurting…"

"Good day!" said the old lady, wearing the same outfit Corvus described earlier, while pointing a shotgun at them. "And why are you two trespassing on my property?"

Corvus let out a scream and Janine jumped in fright, not realizing that someone was there with a gun barrel pointing at the both of them.

"Is there a reason why you are both hiding behind a water trough?"

Corvus and Janine looked at each other and nodded their heads in agreement.

The old lady examined the crow's and Janine's faces. "By the way, my name is Ema and what are the both of you doing here? There is nothing here to steal, so what do you want?"

"Um…what was the first question?" asked Corvus. He then noticed that the old lady was not impressed with his remark. "Well, you see it was like this…"

Janine interrupted the crow by putting her hand up as if she was in school, but quickly realized she was in the wrong place and the wrong time, and immediately put her hand down as both Corvus and the old lady looked at her.

"Look, I better introduce myself properly. My name is Janine and I was chosen to find Snow Sleeper or, the snow queen."

Noticing she was not getting any response from Ema, she continued.

"Yes! Well, Um...apparently, I was the chosen one and the old tree, what I mean is that J. Regia mentioned you would be the person I should speak to, to help me find the snow queen and Corvus showed me how to reach your place. But, see, that's the funny thing. I already know about your place, so I am a bit confused why J. Regia did not say Uncle Tom's farmhouse in the first place, because I would have known exactly how to get here without all this secret stuff and detours!"

"She may have had a reason for all of this, but to tell you the truth, I have been expecting you," said the old woman. "But I wasn't sure what was behind the trough until I met you both. I was startled, and by the look of your faces, you were too. Anyway, get up from there and come inside the barn before you catch your death of cold."

"Well, you know you scared us," mumbled Corvus. He almost fell over while he was fluffing his feathers and cleaning himself in the snow. "You old windbag."

"I heard that!" shouted the old lady.

Janine turned around, and Corvus and her exchanged glances as he raised his eyebrows with disgust and followed the old lady. The three of them headed towards the old barn.

Once entered, the aroma of the cattle dung became quite nauseating and Corvus almost fainted from the odor, but he was able to retrieve his footing when Janine gave him her scarf to mask the smell. Janine also placed her hand over her nose to endure the stench until she was able to tolerate it.

They tagged along with the old lady until they came to an old wooden door with a large latch. The old lady used the butt of the shotgun to undo the latch without too much of a struggle. As the door creaked open, the old lady walked towards a cluttered counter full of tools. The dust was everywhere and cobwebs were making permanent homes at each corner of the walls. Janine started to sneeze as she removed her hand from her mouth and hoped that she was not going to stay long in this filthy room. Corvus also removed the scarf from his head and slowly sniffed the air in the small room and finally accepted the fact he was able to withstand the foul odor.

The old lady laid down the shotgun, picked up a rusty, tin can from the shelf above the counter, and sat on a wooden bench as she used one of her husband's screwdrivers to pry open the dusty can. Once the lid was opened, a sparkle of gold dust appeared into the air and suddenly, like magic, the room changed into a pleasant workroom. Her hand reached into the can and pulled out a white cloth filled with shelled nuts. Instantly, Janine recognized that they were walnuts.

It was then the old lady handed Janine the white cloth with the nuts and said, "This is for you! You need to take these to help you with your mission. They were just picked this fall and I carefully shelled these walnuts so they would not break in half for this special occasion. Be careful not to lose them because they will come in handy."

After looking at the walnuts for a short while, Janine placed them in the tin can carefully. She thanked the old lady for the walnuts and took the rusty, tin can into her hands as Ema said, "My dear, you cannot take this special tin can with you on your journey because it will be too hard to handle. You must carry the nuts a different way. Here. You may use this small bag with a drawstring, which I used to hold my marbles with when I was a little girl. It will be a lot easier to carry." Ema went through a drawer, underneath the counter, and gave Janine a tiny velvet bag. Janine again carefully transferred the white cloth with the walnuts into the small marble bag, drew the strings tight so that none of the walnuts would fall out, and placed them in one of the deep pockets of her coat.

8

Just as Janine was ready to leave, she decided that she had to ask Ema a question. "Can you tell me why I need to take these walnuts with me?"

"You have a long journey ahead of you, Janine, and along the way you may need some encouragement. These walnuts are to be used only as a remedy when you have an anxiety attack. When you do not feel well and become scared about something, take one full walnut and chew it thoroughly. It will dissolve instantly and you should feel the effects soon after. They have a magical ingredient in them and they will not harm you. Now, I gave you enough for your trip, but do not waste them, because when you feel that you may need them, you may not have enough to help you along the rest of the way."

As the old lady picked up her shotgun, Janine and Corvus were ushered out of the room and began to walk towards the exit when Janine mumbled her question as to what was the direction they had to take to find the snow queen. The old lady asked them both to stop so that she could put her shotgun by the door. She also wanted to make sure the directions were clear for Janine and Corvus to understand.

"Before you leave this farm, I must tell you that your mission will not be an easy one because obstacles will come your way and you must find a way to surpass any and all dilemmas, but before you get too concerned, Corvus will help you decide the right path and be your guide. He had been given instructions from J. Regia for this journey and with his intelligence and cautiousness, you must trust him, for he will not lead you astray.

"Please be off before you think about it more, Janine. And whatever you do, do not lose those walnuts."

"I promise. But can you tell me where am I going?"

"Of course, follow me out of the barn and I will direct you to where the snow queen may rest during the winter season."

Janine and the old lady walked out of the barn and found Corvus perched on a fence post nearby, spreading his wings while mumbling to himself. As they came closer they overheard the crow ask, "How can anyone stand the smell of this dump? It will take me days to get rid of this putrid stench. Why me? What did I do to deserve all this?" Corvus sniffed his body with disgust, "I am going to have to find a place to go and bathe in baking soda. Yuck!"

"After a while you get use to it. It's not so bad. Don't be so hard on yourself, Corvus," Ema said.

"Easy for you to say. You lose your sense of smell with age. Among other things."

"Now, now, Corvus, be nice. I did not lose my sense of smell; you get use to it after you have tended the animals in the barn for so long. There's no need to get rude at this point. You have a mission to complete, remember? Stay focused." The old lady patted him on the head.

"Ah, trouble! Trouble always finds me and I wish it would find someone else for a change."

"Now listen up you two, I am only going to tell you this once. Snow Sleeper, as known as…"

"The snow queen," interrupted Janine.

"Exactly! The snow queen is probably in hiding and being protected by Snow Scandiaca, also known as her guardian."

"Who or what is Snow Scandiaca or the guardian?" asked Janine.

"Snow Scandiaca is the snowy owl, the guardian. He is faithful to her and he would give his life to protect her at all cost. This is why I find it odd that Snow Scandiaca is not keeping up with his end of the bargain to assist the snow queen with her duties. Her absence has been too long. It is possible that he too may be in danger and needs some support. I am hoping that both of you will be on time to find her and Snow Scandiaca before it is too late for the animals and birds.

"I suppose that you have also heard of Faeran. You must outwit Faeran, the evil phantom, during your task because he will try to prevent you from completing your mission. Faeran has friends, but don't forget" (as Ema hugged Janine) "Corvus will watch over you. Use your instincts and don't forget your walnuts!"

The comfort from the old lady's arms was warm and sincere, which Janine had not felt in a long time. Corvus too walked up to Janine and stood by her side, acknowledging the fact that he will support her. This type of encouragement mentally helped her get through this difficult assignment, which she knew had to be done. It was then she pointed out, "Thank you, Ema and Corvus. Your assistance and comfort means a lot to me."

"Your welcome, Janine," replied Ema.

"I will protect you, Janine. I promise," remarked Corvus

"You have no idea how much it means to me to be the chosen one and to have met some nice acquaintances along the way. It certainly makes one feel better to be encouraged to conclude this important mission."

"We are aware of your feelings, but because of your interest in animals and birds, we felt you were the one," Ema said.

"What are your instructions, and which way do we go?" Janine asked. "I want to get this over with!"

"Me, too," said Corvus. "I would love to sun myself in…"

"Listen carefully, children. It is a two-mile, or is it three?

"Which is it: two or three?" Corvus asked. "I can't take all this abuse. Not only did she lose her sense of smell, but her sense of direction too. Make up your mind. I am dying out here. Get a whiff of me. Whoa, mama! I can't stand myself."

"I'm getting to it. Hold your horses. It is two miles. I am sure of that. You must cross over to the other side of the railroad tracks until you come across a wooded, rocky hill near a lake. Corvus will be your compass, Janine. He must fly due south and you must follow him at all cost. When you see Snow Scandiaca, it is then you are close to the snow queen. From that point on, Snow Scandiaca will be your escort; that is, if he's all right."

As they all walked back to the trough, the old lady laid down her shotgun and said, "I must go now. Tom will be waking up soon from his afternoon nap, and he always caresses the pillow next to him and I want to be there. Goodbye and good luck."

"Can I ask you one more question, Ema?" Janine blurred, as she knew she kept Corvus waiting.

"Sure. Shoot."

"Why are you carrying a shotgun when there is no need to?" Janine wondered.

"Just a habit. That is all!" said the old lady with a smile.

"Oh! Okay."

As the old lady picked up her shotgun by the trough and headed towards the farmhouse, she lifted the 16-gauge in the air as a wave when Janine and Corvus said their goodbyes.

A decision had to be made as to which path would be the best route to take while they traveled south. As Corvus flew up in the air, it was not long until Janine realized she had to trust Corvus and that it was going to be a long trudge against all odds to find the snow queen. But first she noticed that dusk was approaching fast and that they soon would be facing complete darkness in the lonely forest.

9

Keeping a watchful eye on Corvus above, Janine maneuvered her gait quite well, but at times she still had to stop and empty her snow-filled boots. For just a few seconds, Janine wondered: will the weather prevent them from completing their mission, and will the shadows she had been seeing every once in awhile affect her task?

As Janine was thinking of all this, Corvus shouted from above, "Hey! Let's get a move on! We have a long day ahead of us. Let's make the best of it while there is still some daylight left. Yuck. It's probably best that I am up here because I really need to air out my feathers. Others may take offence to my unpleasant odor. Or not! Who knows, I may attract the undesirables. Just my luck! It is going to take awhile until…"

"Corvus! Stick with the program and quit muttering to yourself! Get over it! We must focus. Are you with me?"

"Yes, mademoiselle, at your service mademoiselle. At your beck and call, mademo…"

"Don't get saucy with me, Corvus. I am just trying to get you to stop complaining all the time. You tend to get carried away with yourself. Have you been like this all your living life?"

"I don't know. Maybe?"

"You are so use to grumbling that you don't even notice it. Shall we move on or should I wait until you are finished?"

"Wow, someone got up on the wrong side of the bed. Yes, let us move on. Can you see me clearly?"

"Yes!"

"Good. Because once we reach the forest, you must constantly look up and watch where you are going. Shout at me if I am going too fast, so that you will not get behind."

Janine could see that he was anxious to lead while he made headway towards the forest. She too was eager to continue, when all of a sudden Janine felt a vibration close to her body. Making sure that Corvus was still in sight, she carefully unzipped her snowsuit and noticed that Right Whisper was trying to say something to her.

"Janine."

"Hi, Right Whisper. What is it?"

"Just a reminder that if you are in need to talk to someone, I am around. And try not to be too hard on Corvus. He's harmless, but he babbles a lot. Deep down he cares for you."

"Thanks for the advice. I will not be so hard on him next time. Now can I go because Corvus is ahead of me and I do not want to lose him?"

"Yes, child."

"Okay, goodbye," whispered Janine as she bundled herself up and hurried towards the direction of the forest.

"Are you coming?" Corvus shouted. "What's keeping you?"

"Nothing. I was just straightening my snowsuit. Move on and let's go!" She watched Corvus fly towards the forest.

Janine loved the forest and all of its contents. For example, how the snow covered each branch from the fir trees as if it were set for a winter scene picture postcard. She also loved observing the few various winter birds amidst her surroundings. The black-capped chickadees whistling their song in a slow *"Swee-tee-dee-dee,"* as if to say, *"This is all I have left to say, but I will try to cheer things up with my song."* So sad to see such effort made from a small bird, who spends its time flying from branch to branch and shriveling twigs for insects or berries, but finds hardly any.

Generally, throughout winter months, chickadees are often joined with other birds, like the kinglets, nuthatches, creepers, small woodpeckers, and sometimes, boreal chickadees that have a grey-brown cap, back, sides, and flanks. All these small birds scour from branch to branch celebrating the life of the forest, but this time there were none to be found. Janine loved birds because they had always been around her house, singing cheerfully and keeping her company when she would wander in the woods close by. This time, sporadically, the chickadees would sing, but mostly silence was present except for the sound of her movements in the snow and the creaking of the branches as she stepped on them while walking.

She realized that there weren't any paths once she reached the thick of the forest, but she had to focus on Corvus and her instincts of survival at all cost. This raised her heartbeat to where she had to stop thinking of the worst, but Janine's thoughts of worry and fear began to increase as she trudged into the deep of the forest. Knowing very well she was being followed, she tried not to think of being scared since Corvus was near, but fear of the unknown increased her lack of confidence.

As she pushed herself to concentrate on her mission, she could see from the corner of her eye that tall shadows were beginning to enclose her as she decided to take an alternate route. She could feel the tightness in her chest. Tears began to flow down her cheeks as she escalated her speed. The situation intensified and she became conscious of the danger she was in. Just as she was about to shout up above, and not paying attention where she was going, she lost her gait in the snow and fell. It was then that she noticed that she tripped over the railroad tracks.

Looking up, she could not see Corvus and became slightly nervous as to where her next direction should be. Janine decided to call for Corvus and wait for his appearance. While hanging around for a response, she happened to notice an unusual pattern in the snow. Being an inquisitive person, and not paying attention to whether or not Corvus was up above, Janine walked slowly towards the configuration and thought to herself that the design was very artistic. It wasn't until she was smack into the middle of the pattern when immediately Janine felt something wrapped around her feet from underneath the snow and began to pull her. In a few seconds she was on her back and was being dragged rapidly through the forest.

Janine could not untie what was wrapped around her ankles since she was being swiftly towed through the thick, bushy snow. Holding on to her snowsuit tightly, she tried to call for help, but the snow held her back as she gasped and coughed for air. Then, all of a sudden, *Whoosh!*

Janine was suddenly falling feet first, down a crevice of some kind. She failed to warn Corvus that she has been abducted. Falling helplessly, she suddenly landed on a somewhat semihard surface.

"Ouch! Oh, that hurt." She laid there for a while trying to figure out what had just happened to her.

Trying to calm down, Janine's body ached all over. With limited daylight from above, she began to unravel the rope that was around her ankles.

She thrashed about and got back on her feet. It was then she noticed meager-size human beings, about a foot-and-a-half tall, with torn clothing, mangled short hair, and small ears. Their tiny black eyes were not centered correctly, nor were their large mouths. All of them had small hands and feet, which surrounded her as she finally stood up. With her heart pounding, she screamed and felt ill. Troubled as to what would happen to her next, she could hear the small figures laughing, and instinctively Janine began to shout Corvus' name several times, with the word "help" in between.

Meanwhile, up above, Corvus did keep a watchful eye on Janine below and noticed that she had disappeared. Unable to rescue her on time, he decided to perch himself on a nearby tree from where she vanished. He knew that sooner or later something would emerge from the site to cover their tracks where Janine disappeared.

Sure enough, minutes later, a figure, cloaked in white, moved ever so cautiously from the hole where Janine disappeared and checked to see if anyone or anything was watching. Unbeknownst to the creature below, Corvus was observing the figure's movements and was ready to strike at any moment.

As the distorted creature turned its head away, Corvus took the opportunity to use his sharp talons on the small creature in one swift swoop. Struggling hard to escape from Corvus' grip, the being could not free itself from the crow's strong hold. It tried to scream, but Corvus, being heavy, strong, and tall, outweighed the creature and held it by its neck so tightly that it could not call for assistance. He knew what he was doing and made sure no one saw the incident.

In the meantime, Janine looked up to see if she could escape by making an attempt to climb from the hole she was dragged into. She was abruptly distracted by a faint sound that was coming from the inside of her snowsuit. Realizing that it was Right Whisper who was calling her, she could hardly make out what was being said because of the chanting noise from the creatures below. As Janine removed her mitts, she unzipped her snowsuit to speak to Right Whisper, but she was seized by several of the creatures by her arms and legs. Struggling and screaming to free herself, she felt lifeless and could not liberate herself from their strong hold. Their little hands hoisted her up and quickly removed her from the place she landed.

Darkness fell quickly as they moved downward into the hollow cavity of the earth. Janine was unable to see what was going on, but continued to thrash about and attempt to free herself in any way she could. Feeling their tiny fingers holding her ever so firmly, she was unsuccessful at escaping.

Up above, Corvus needed a private area to interrogate the creature as to the whereabouts of Janine. Necessary force was going to be needed in order to extract the information he required from the captive. Finally, he found a secluded location proper for questioning and landed on an abandoned Cooper's hawk's nest. Holding on to the creature with one of his claws, he turned the being around to face him with both of his talons on the distorted figure's chest and questioned it.

"Now that you are alone with me to contend with, where are your friends taking the little girl you captured? And who are you anyway?"

As the tiny black eyes starred at Corvus with hatred, the creature did not answer.

Corvus repeated himself adding a little more pressure onto the creature's chest.

The distorted figure winced and said, "I do not know what you are talking about. I was just minding my own business when…"

Corvus dug his talons deeper into the creature's body and could feel the victim flinch with pain.

"I am not going to ask you again. Where is she?"

"What if I do not tell you? You cannot do anything to me. If you kill me then you will not be able to find out where the little girl is. Besides, the others will notice."

"They will notice nothing. Especially when they cannot find you. Have you ever seen a crow mutilate its victim?"

Corvus brought the creature closer to his face; the creature shook its head no.

"Well, you see, they hold on to their victim like so," as his grip dug in deeper. "And then they spear their bill into their upper body like so…"

"No, no. Please stop!" begged the creature. "I will tell you! Please do not hurt me!"

"Speak! Now!" demanded Corvus.

10

As she was being carried deeper into the cave, Janine wondered where the creatures were taking her and where they came from all of a sudden? Were these the shadows that followed her from the beginning of her journey? Hopefully, she would live to find out.

Now, she was in a dilemma and was behind her schedule in finding the snow queen. With all this jostling about, she was sick to her stomach with the whole thing and was afraid of what these creatures had in store for her. At that point she could not help but trade her confidence for a feeling of helplessness. She needed to stay calm because she was not sure what was in store ahead.

Finally, the creatures stopped and lowered her down on an opened space of a cave.

Janine could vaguely see because the cave was only illuminated with dim lights, which were lit by fireflies in large closed jam jars. The roots from trees added character to the cave.

She immediately stood up and noticed that these small, disfigured creatures surrounded her. All was still. Not a sound was made. The creatures just starred at Janine and began to form a tight circle around her. And because she was taller than they, she was able to finally see what was nearby. It was then she was looking for an escape route. The cave had many avenues, but which was the right one to take?

She noticed that the roots from the trees above were rather peculiar. Beautiful archways decorated by the fireflies in jars and the taproots from the trees above were the foundations of the cave. She also observed that there were some areas of the rocky walls of the cave that were sharp in places and dismal. If anyone were to lean on them, they would definitely be injured.

There were many paths in the bleak cavern, but she knew that it was time to take action. So, she decided to question the perpetrators. "Who are you people and why have you taken me hostage?"

She anxiously waited for an answer, but there was no response; only a low hum sound was emitted from the creatures.

"This is not funny. I want to get out of here and you won't let me. Why?" asked Janine. "I was innocently walking in the woods when you guys" (as she pointed her finger at them) "attacked me."

Noticing that the creatures were still ignoring her, she spoke softly to herself. "Obviously, they are not listening to me. I must find a way out of here. Soon. Real soon."

With everything around her going on, she simply forgot about Right Whisper until, once again, she heard a murmur underneath her snowsuit. Instantly, she went into the secret compartment of her snowsuit while the strange beings continued to gawk at her.

Right Whisper reminded Janine to check to see if the bag the old lady gave her was still on her person. She obeyed, and sure enough, despite all that hard traveling, she had held on to the marble bag.

With Right Whisper's direction, she quickly unraveled the bag and chose a piece to eat from the bag's contents. She chewed on the piece of walnut, which tasted like sweet caramel, but did not stick to her teeth; it dissolved almost instantaneously in her mouth. The creatures ceased their tedious droning sound. All eyes were on Janine and their bodies stood motionless. She watched them cautiously as she swallowed, wondering why they acted so peculiar.

"Give me that!" A skeletal elongated finger with long sharp nails from behind her abruptly clasped the bag. Janine trembled when the phantom uttered in a deep hoarse voice, "What is this? Some candy for a scared little girl?"

Janine zipped up her snowsuit. When she slowly turned around she saw a tall, eerie, dark, and ghostly beast with a white glow surrounding its body, but no recognizable features, except deep-orange eyes that glared at her. The only thing that covered this ghost was its black robe along with long sleeves and a black hood, which revealed its head. Hovering over her body, the phantom tossed the bag to the other side of the cave and cackled as if it were a joke. The tiny figures followed suit, except for a few who fought for the bag. The phantom finally stopped laughing and so did the creatures, all examining the little girl carefully.

Janine suddenly felt a chill go right through her, with her heart pounding in her eardrums. What were they up to and why were they so interested in her? She wondered how Corvus would ever reach her in the cave and if he would notice that she was missing?

She would need to get out of the cave, and, when the opportunity arrives, she will have to elude her enemies somehow and then get away from them. The problem was the phantom, which seemed to have her frozen with intimidation.

"Unzip your coat, little girl! At once!" demanded the phantom.

"Snowsuit," said Janine nervously.

"Whatever!" the phantom retorted. But Janine obeyed immediately and found herself in even more trouble when the phantom removed Right Whisper from her person. Another additional problem was added to her getaway plan. When will the right time come, she wondered?

"Well, well, well. What have we got here?" inquired the phantom while assessing the item. "I have never seen this before. It must be a new mirror, and of some value to you or else you would not carry it with you all this time. Speak up, girl! I do not have all day! I have a lot of work to do and I do not have the patience to tolerate your silence!"

The tone was one that the small creatures knew too well as they lowered their heads not to disappoint the phantom while it was aggravated.

Janine could tell that these small creatures were afraid of something, as the phantom's shadowy mass looked over the congregation. As Janine was about to answer, the phantom interrupted her yet again and passed Right Whisper to one of the two taller guards who were holding long spears.

"I will give you a chance to think for a moment," said the phantom. "Let me introduce myself. I am Faeran, and these are my children. I provide them with a home, responsibility, comfort, food, shelter et cetera, et cetera, et cetera. They are well provided for, but enough about them. What is your name, little girl?"

"My name is Janine. And I demand to know why you captured me and treated me like a criminal? I almost suffocated earlier when your little creatures dragged me across the snow. Why am I here, and where the heck am I?"

"So many questions, for a foreigner. Now... which one of these lovely creatures treated you so badly?" asked Faeran as he mocked Janine in front of the congregation.

"How did you know that I am a foreigner?"

"I know everything!" exclaimed Faeran.

"So why did you asked for my name if you know everything?"

"Just direct me to the guilty party!"

As Janine examined the creatures more carefully she had difficulty in recognizing who abducted her. They all looked the same: small, gnarled facial features with what seemed to be arthritic small feet and hands, and pointed ears. Quite frightening looking creatures actually. In a way she felt sorry for them because of their appearance.

"I am not sure exactly, but that is not the point."

"Not sure! Surely, you do not accuse my lovely creatures of a crime when you cannot identify them. Is it this one" (as the phantom, with a strong white glow encircling him, glided towards one of the creatures) "or this one, or is it that one?" The little creatures laughed at Janine.

She gave no answer.

"Just as I thought! No concrete evidence. It is not polite to point the finger at someone if you are not sure if they did it. Did your mother or father not teach you to be responsible for your own actions before blaming others? Around here, it is an offence to accuse someone without proof and the punishment for this is severe." Faeran hovered near Janine.

"I take it that it will be you who would give out the sentence?" asked Janine.

Faeran evaluated his captive carefully and laughed. "Of course. Even though these little ones are quite capable of looking after themselves, they need guidance, provided that they follow my orders and can distinguish a dignified leader such as myself who would be able to take good care of them for a very, very long time."

"Did they come at their own free will, like I did?"

"Enough!" screeched the phantom. "For a frightened little girl, you sure have a lot to say and are quite mouthy I might say. You need to have your mouth washed out with soap or something like that. I am not about to play games with you, Janine, so I will place you under surveillance for a while until I decide what to do with you. In the meantime, you will follow my direct orders" (as he motioned the two tall guards to escort Janine to one of the avenues of the cave) "and not give me any more trouble. Is that understood?"

Janine noticed that the two tall guards were not identical to each other, nor did they resemble the small creatures. They were around five feet tall, and wore black robes with hoods, white sashes around their waists, knives in their sashes, and carried long spears with gold tips. Their fingers were long with knobby tips. Janine could not see their feet or their eyes.

As the two guards headed towards Janine, one said, "Janine, either you come with us quietly or we will have to carry you to your confinement."

"You are bullies and I will not obey you!" Janine shouted, but noticed that their voices were young.

""Then you leave us no choice," answered one of the guards."

Janine struggled with the two guards as they swept her of her feet and forced her down one of the tunnels of the cave.

"You have no right to keep me here, you idiotic nincompoops. I did not do anything to get punished like this. You are mean and one day something will happen to you for what you do to people. Let me go! You have no right!"

Janine began to flail. Fighting for her life, she felt that it was a lost cause to struggle with the two strong protectors. For she felt that they too were in grave danger if they did not follow orders. It seemed that the phantom had power over everyone in the cave and was not going to allow any mistakes to happen. So the guards had to fulfill their instructions without any complication in order to survive.

Her thoughts were racing now, and she was afraid of what might happen to her, especially after the phantom threatened her.

Not paying any attention to where the guards were taking her, she continued to kick and fight back as much as she could, but realized that her strength was beginning to fade away. She was tired and angry, and on top of it all, being manhandled by strange beings.

Finally, the guards tossed her into a small section of the cave where long, lanky roots from the trees above were jumbled everywhere. When one of the guards pointed his spear towards Janine to prevent her from escaping, the other guard with precision touched the tips of the roots to imprison Janine. When she tried to break out, she accidentally laid a hand on one of the tips of a root and it too began to grow slowly around her thigh. She panicked and immediately stopped the root from growing by refraining from touching it. The guards snickered and left her behind.

Janine wondered what her next move was and how was she going to remove the stem of the root from her body without accidentally touching the tip. Then she had an idea. Since the stem was wrapped around her snowsuit, maybe with patience and accuracy she could remove her snowsuit off her body without falling victim to the root. It was worth a shot.

All those dancing lessons she took since she was seven should help out with her agility. She knew that it was going to take a while, but she had to free herself. At the back of her mind she could only use her snowsuit as refuge, avoiding any skin connection to the tip of the main root. So the process began.

Finally, with some close calls, Janine managed to remove her snowsuit off her body one section at a time while balancing from one foot to the other. She was then liberated, but had to leave her snowsuit and boots inside the circle of the root.

Janine also noticed that a couple of lanterns filled with fireflies illuminated her room. On the other end of her room, she noticed a small ragged cot with no pillow or sheets. As she was inspecting her imprisonment with great caution, finding no way out, she suddenly felt a weird sensation filtering throughout her body. It was as if a new source of emotional energy surged into her soul, giving her unlimited confidence she had never felt before.

Without a moment to lose, Janine again studied her room and made a decision to carefully act out her escape plan. First, she decided to carry the fireflies with her so that she would have a source of light as she made her way through the cavern. Next, she gently removed her snowsuit and boots from the stem and used her scarf to maneuver the tips of the roots to give her enough room to escape. Then, she pulled out the cot as a guide between the roots and herself so that she was able to squeeze out of her confinement with her snowsuit and boots on. Finally, Janine grabbed the fireflies from under the cot and continued to search for a way out of the cave where she could escape and find Corvus.

As Faeran sat comfortably on his throne with his two guards by his side, he carefully examined Right Whisper. He paid no attention to the small creatures busily maintaining the cave or eating the bugs from one another. Placing it gently on the side table, the phantom began to rock back and forth in the chair, contemplating what to do with the mirror and with the newest member of his congregation. He couldn't decide whether she would be his personal slave or work in the caves for the rest of her life.

Just then, a sharp pain interrupted his thoughts, and at that moment, he began to feel ill and had no desire to make a decision of her fate as of yet. It was time for the phantom to be somewhere else, which needed attending to. More importantly, gratification needed to be focused on, so that the phantom's existence may continue.

"I have a reputation to maintain and I need to scout out there once again to gain the strength I deserve. Keep a watchful eye on the little girl and do not fail me in keeping her here until I get back. Do I make myself clear?" he addressed the two guards.

Without looking at their leader, the guards and the small, distorted creatures all nodded their heads with acknowledgement except for one. It was then Faeran noticed the loner by the corner of the cave and asked, "You there, did you hear what I said or are you deaf?" The small creature disguised in white was not facing the phantom, but kept busy by attending to the fireflies. Quickly, it acknowledged the command and waved. The phantom was nearing the loner by the corner when, without warning, he cringed with pain once again. Seeing that everyone was watching and trying not to lose face, the phantom decided to vacate without delay. For he knew everyone who feared him would increase his power and would have no choice but to obey his command.

He then evaporated into thin air.

11

Immediately, the guards and creatures left their posts and headed about their own business. They began to perform their chores by looking after the cave and the fireflies, and the guards went back to guarding the entrance of Janine's compartment. It was then the loner by the corner discreetly left the others and disappeared down one of the avenues of the cave. While the guards walked towards their captive with their spears in hand, they both thought they heard a noise not far behind. Looking around, both checked to see if anyone was there, but quickly gave up when they saw nothing. They finally reached Janine's cell when they noticed her absence. They knew not to panic and had to find her immediately.

"After being warned by the phantom to keep a watchful eye on her, I am not prepared to face the consequences for this," said one of the guards.

"We must find her before Faeran comes back," said the other.

So, off they went to search for the little girl.

Janine was not far from the two guards, hiding the lanterns behind her back, when she unintentionally ran into a creature that was even smaller than the others.

"Ah! Get your hands off of me," Janine screamed as she fought against her unknown attacker.

"Janine, be quiet. It's me," said Corvus as he struggled with Janine.

With mouth agape, Janine was happy to see her friend and hugged him.

"How did you find me in this horrible place?"

"It is a long story and I will tell you later, but now let us skedaddle out of here."

This time the guards did hear a definite sound and scurried towards it. They then found Janine and Corvus and began to pursue them. After a very short chase, Corvus found a good hiding place in the cave.

"This way," whispered Corvus to Janine as he led the way.

"No, no, Corvus. We must find Right Whisper and the bag of walnuts first."

"Do you know how hard it was for me to put on this ridiculous white outfit with these feathers in the way and make my way into this hole without being caught? They just had to look at my feet and my beak and WHAO LA! I could just hear them say, 'Hey! He is not one of us! Now is he?' Then he continued, "Get my drift? I am making an effort here right now for us to disappear from this place and you want to play hide and seek."

"I know, I know, but I will protect what is rightly mine and no one is going to take that away from me. Not even what's his name!"

"Fearium. Or was it Fairan."

"Whatever," stammered Janine.

"Where do we start, oh wondrous one, and what were you planning to do with those?" He pointed to the fireflies.

"We stay together and we try to find the phantom's room. I feel that Right Whisper is in there and probably the marble bag too," said Janine.

Corvus shook his head. "Why me? Why was I so fortunate to be the chosen one? Why can this not be a simple case of…?"

"Quit complaining and get on with it, boy! I certainly was never allowed to complain at home or else…"

"Yes, but you sure made up for it by back talking."

"Corvus, let's go. You can complain later."

"Okay. I know the way."

"How do you know where to go?"

"Quiet! Stay close to me so that you won't get lost and you may just as well place those lanterns here with the others so that we may use them on our way out."

Janine obeyed and off they went en route.

They cautiously made their way towards the phantom's domain when they encountered two of the small creatures guarding his room; noticing that the original two guards were nowhere to be seen, Janine decided to sneak behind them after discussing with Corvus first. So he followed her. She wrapped her hand around one of the creature's mouths, and dragged it into the phantom's room. The victim squiggled viciously and tried to escape through Janine's grip but failed. Corvus, being a strong crow for his size, pounced onto the other guard, grabbed it by the collar of the outfit it wore, and tightened his grip so it could not scream. It too struggled but was unsuccessful in escaping. He then dragged it into the room so the others would not be aware of what had happened to them. Janine had already tied up her captive with some cloth she found in the room.

Quickly, she did the same to the other creature that Corvus had captured. Then Janine started to search for her items, but without success. Corvus too looked in every nook and cranny, but could not find anything.

Suddenly, Janine realized she was not alone in the phantom's room and was at once surrounded by a throng of small creatures. Looking for a way out, she yelled at the creatures, "Move or I will pop you all!" The creatures only laughed at her loudly and stood steadfast.

The two guards, who had been searching for her, finally arrived and were about to grab her when Janine bellowed out her threat again. There was nothing but silence in the room except talking between the two guards.

Corvus had to come up with a quick plan. He motioned the guards to stop and told the creatures and the guards that he was unable to control Janine, and that he also trembled with fear when she lost her temper and would not like to be around if she did. That was why he had to follow her orders.

Janine soon picked up on his plan, walked up to him, and threw him across the floor. The others watched in horror and made no attempt to catch her. Something had changed her. According to them she was dangerous and would hurt them. Corvus pretended to be knocked out and peaked through one eye to see if Janine was still in control of the situation. Sure enough, she was.

Janine rapidly walked over and grabbed a small creature by the neck and demanded her valuables.

"Please spare us," said one of the small creatures. "We will obey you."

"Be quiet. Do you wish more punishment from your leader?" said one of the guards.

"No. But we do not want her to harm us either," said another creature. "Just imagine what the phantom will do to you if he found out she escaped while you were on duty. And besides, have you not noticed her present inner strength?"

Everyone was starring at Janine for a second or two when at last she spoke. "That's better. Now where are they?" Janine kept a strong hold onto the small creature for insurance.

Only one squeaked from the lineup and pointed to the direction as to the whereabouts of the contents.

"No, no. That is too easy. One of you go and get it for me and if you drop it, your friend here will be very sorry that it happened!" she hollered.

"No! No! Please! We are only slaves of Faeran. Do not harm us. Please," most of them shrieked.

It was then she noticed that all of the small creatures lowered their heads, but the guards glared at her with disgust. A creature, who was chosen by the congregation, walked slowly towards the location of the goods and searched. The only item it could find was Right Whisper. It immediately began to panic.

"I…I am sorry, Janine, but I do not know where the bag is," the creature said.

"Please…please do not hurt our friend. It was not our fault," said another.

The others muttered amongst themselves.

Janine took it to heart what the small creature had said, but also noticed something strange above her head. Rubbing her eyes, she looked again and was quite disturbed at what she saw: images of young children, crying for help without sound.

Looking at the creatures with uncertainty she questioned them. "Who are you little people? Where do you come from?"

As one tried to respond to her questions, another creature nudged it, nodding its head no.

"Fine, do not answer me. See if I care! Now what seems to be the problem with finding my other parcel?"

"I...can only find this mirror, but no parcel. It was here the last time."

Not wasting any more time, Corvus decided to gradually get up and assist Janine.

Acting as if he was unbalanced on his feet, he made his way to a dark area so that no one could make out his features. Being an observant person, Janine knew her time was up and Corvus was ready to depart shortly. She grabbed Right Whisper in one hand and held on to the other creature, running-towards the direction Corvus was leading her.

She could not help but think of how miserable she felt in leaving the small creatures behind when she looked at their disgruntled and gloomy faces as if they were ready to cry. Something was horribly wrong. It was quite evident that these small creatures were prisoners themselves and had no way out or hopes to live a normal life of their own. Could it be that the phantom had the power to remove their frightened souls out of their bodies and held them as prisoners? He seemed to feed on human fear. Is that why they were to be seen on the ceiling and not heard? It is as if they were incomplete beings. She also noticed that they did not show any aggression as she exited the phantom's room. Without hesitation, she released the small creature and said she was sorry that she had to handle it with force. The impression the small, distorted creature had bestowed upon her left an imprint of sadness on her heart. Janine had to think of something to save these small beings, but how?

Janine promised the little creature that she would be back to help them escape from the dreadful place and also mentioned not to forget to release the two that were tied up in the room. She wanted them to feel that they will not be forgotten.

Seemingly, Corvus had it all mapped out, and in a short while, they were back to where the two lanterns were placed previously. Janine questioned Corvus as to the location they were at, but Corvus assured her that she must trust him. Not making any fuss over the whole situation, she wanted out of this dungeon, as soon as possible, with the help of the fireflies.

Satisfied with Janine's response over what course to take, he immediately led her to the route he had come from. For he, too, wanted out and knew that if they did not leave the cave at once, they would not be able to save the winter season, thus leaving Janine's soul to the phantom's delight. Corvus would not be able to forgive himself if he failed and lost Janine to such a fate. The constant desire of courage and persistence was strong at the moment, which fulfilled his determination to succeed, even though he knew they were in grave danger. Although Janine's attitude was great for them at the time, he knew it was only temporary. It would only be a matter of time before the phantom would return and recognize that she had escaped and would have to be retrieved.

To his surprise footsteps from the guards were getting closer, so he carefully led the way.

Knowing that the fireflies may die outside of the cave, Janine positioned them on a ledge nearby and let them go. She said her goodbyes, hoping that one day they too would escape this dreadful place of confinement. Keeping up with the crow, she quickly hastened her gait and copied Corvus' steps.

Trying to look into the morning light again was painful, but soon her eyes adjusted to the bright light; she realized that it was morning.

Time was running out.

12

Stumbling a few times, Janine finally found her bearings when she realized that she was no longer in the cave.

Noting that they were falling behind in their mission, she knew they had to hurry and, with haste, they left the dreadful place. She was able to see Corvus clearly flying overhead, but realized that fresh snow had fallen during her time in the cave, giving her a harder time with mobility. She wanted to achieve so badly and run away from that horrible ghost that she had forgotten how cumbersome the two feet of snow had become. Janine also realized a change was happening inside her body. The mission seemed to weigh her down, giving her a negative attitude about their present and future circumstances. The fear of failing was apparent.

Once again, Janine was back to her old self and hated every minute of it. Her self-confidence was in jeopardy. What was happening to her? Will someday all of this go away as she matured and change?

Corvus kept an eye on Janine as he headed south and noticed that she was always looking behind her when she should have been focusing on what was ahead of her. He knew the phantom was not far. Encouraging Janine to stay on task, he shouted, "Come on, Janine, hurry up and never mind as to what is behind you. I will let you know if you are being followed! Just keep up the pace and I will direct you to safety soon. Trust me!"

"Like the last time? Easy for you to say," Janine mumbled as she was trudging through the deep snow and brush.

"What did you say?"

"Nothing! You keep on going, and I'll try to follow you as best as I can!"

Right Whisper endlessly thanked Janine from inside Janine's snowsuit for saving her. "Thank you, Janine, for saving me. I was afraid that Faeran would destroy our communication, but he had other matters to attend to. It was a lucky break."

"You are welcome," Janine responded.

Janine trudged through the fresh snow with a decent speed, and Corvus knew that she was doing the best she could under the circumstances. It was not until sometime much later that they were on track when she realized that the ground was somewhat level compared to the previous terrain. Falling into more or less bad visibility, she noticed the terrain was slightly different and flat, opposed to what she was accustomed to. Familiar tall, cluttered grass that grew in marshes during the spring was several feet from where she was standing. As she moved on, she came across a large clearing where there were no reeds or grass at all. Cautiously, she encouraged herself to move forward, but before she was about to change her mind as to where she was going, she decided to call the crow for a new direction.

"Corvus! I think I am walking through…" Just as she yelled at the crow, abruptly she fell through the ice.

"Ahh! Help!" She sputtered and began thrashing her arms in the cold, icy water. The body of water was rising from underneath her and her boots were weighing her down.

Every time she tried to free herself, the ice would break and the water around her was getting wider and wider. She was having difficulty breathing and was incapable of rescuing herself. Janine was desperate and knew that if help were not on its way, she would perish. Her body was getting weaker and weaker, and she tried to mutter for help but could not speak clearly.

It was not until a few seconds after her muttering when, surprisingly, she felt this sensation underneath her arms. Janine was then picked up like a rag doll into the air and set down upon layers and layers of coniferous branches on top of a tall tree. Slightly dazed from the flight, she was not able to grasp what had happened to her at that moment. Where was she and where was Corvus? What happened to his loyalty earlier when he said, "trust me?" Was he close by and did he see what took place a few seconds ago?

Trying to keep her balance on the fir tree as it swayed, she realized she was quite high off the ground. It was a good thing that she was not afraid of heights and that the branches were quite thick and full to hang on to, simultaneously insulating her body from the freezing cold air. Although her legs and feet in particular were numb, with all of the bouncing around, she began to feel a painful tingle. That was a good sign because it meant that Janine's blood circulation was in motion.

These were no ordinary trees, for they were walking with ease in the snow. They seemed to have a great deal of power, maneuvering their solid dark trunks and roots with some flexibility. They did not speak much among themselves, but seemed to know exactly what their next move was. All Janine had to do was hold on to the limbs and not fall off.

"Hold on, Janine, I am right next to you. Do not let go of the branches!" Corvus yelled.

"What did you say about trust and safety, Corvus? I trusted you and look where I just ended up. How come it only happens to me?" bellowed Janine. She began to weep with fear.

"Please do not cry, little girl," said one of the tall coniferous trees that led the way.

"We will put you down once we arrive on solid ground, which will only take a moment. We noticed that you were traveling south and that lands you smack into the wet marsh and deep water. We happened to be nearby when you fell in," said one of the following fir trees. Janine nodded reluctantly, trying to compose herself.

"Corvus! Who are they? And…and where are they taking me? I cannot see where we are going since I…"

"We mean you no harm," said one of the smaller coniferous trees.

"Yup, you seem to attract trouble wherever you go," Corvus said, as he shook his head.

"Never mind what you think. Am I going in the right direction or is there a change of plans right now?" harped Janine, as she tried balancing herself.

"Just hold on tight, and I will follow them as best as I can," shouted Corvus.

He ducked and swooped in and out of the flapping branches while the trees walked with great stride. He was amazed as to the strength these trees were demonstrating as they plunged effortlessly into the marsh, but he was still worried about Janine's safety.

It seemed like it would never end, when at long last the coniferous trees stopped at the water's edge and the leader set Janine down gently. Corvus was exhausted by this time. He flopped down onto the snowy ground to catch his breath. Never had he faced such a feat, to remain in-flight without being knocked down by moving boughs. Luckily, with his air-travel experience from colliding bombs and low flying fighter planes in World War II, he was able to maneuver his pattern of flight with the best of his ability to stay alive. When he flew up into the sky, he was like an acrobat. He was fast, but accurate, to avoid oncoming debris, and because of his experience, bravery, and foresight of danger, he was able to avoid being hit by moving branches with great ease.

"We hope the journey was not too difficult on you, little girl. We try to move as swiftly and steadily as possible, but sometimes we fail," spoke the leader once again, using his windy dialect as they all humbly bowed their heads.

Trying to regain her stability, Janine felt somewhat dizzy and sat down in the snow to recuperate. Not far off, she spotted Corvus mumbling to himself.

"Oh! I almost forgot," she said as she quickly unzipped her snowsuit, "how are you doing Right Whisper? Are you okay?"

With her eyes closed tightly, Right Whisper answered, "Yes, barely."

"Are you all right, Corvus?" yelled Janine.

"All right? Sure. I do this all the time for fun. Who needs a roller coaster when you can play with coniferous trees? I always wanted to be knocked about by branches. It's lot of fun! Are you all right?"

"Yes, I...I think so, but I feel a little wobbly, and surprisingly I am warm and dry," she said as she was trying to stand up. "Can you give me a few minutes before we head off, Corvus?"

"Excuse me," said the leader, noticing that Janine and Corvus were not paying any attention to the trees. "Excuse me!"

"What?" Corvus, Right Whisper, and Janine said simultaneously as they glared at the tree.

"Now that I have your attention, a 'thank you' would be a nice gesture since we saved your life, little girl, but it would seem that you are more involved with your own world and forgetting the importance of the others who helped you," explained one of the smaller coniferous trees.

"Oh. We're sorry. Aren't we Corvus?"

"Sure. Yes. We are truly in your debt," Corvus said while scratching his head. "Sorry for avoiding you."

"Yes, we are truly sorry, aren't we Right Whisper?" Janine said as she became aware of her lack of manners.

"I just said that! Why do you have to repeat the same words? Can't you say something else? Like..." cawed Corvus.

"Like what? I am following your example!" answered Janine.

"Like, we apologize for our ignorance."

"I don't speak like that, ever! Corvus! How old am I, Corvus?"

"You are right. I am an adult and you are a little tur..."

"Don't go any further," she said as she sternly spoke to Corvus with a smirk on her face.

The trees were following the conversation intensely between Corvus and Janine, and moving their branches back and forth to see who would win the argument until Right Whisper stepped in.

"Stop! Both of you stop your kibitzing. All you both had to do was say 'thank you' and leave it at that!" said Right Whisper.

Both Janine and Corvus looked embarrassed when Right Whisper spoke in her soft but firm voice.

"Do you two always speak to each other like this?" asked one of the inquisitive coniferous trees.

"No! Not all the time. Well...sometimes!" muttered Janine as she looked at Corvus. "We do have our moments, don't we Corvus? Corvus? Corvus, answer me!"

Corvus starred at Janine for a second or two and finally said, "We have to go! We have an important...I mean we are out here in the middle of no...well, let's go on with our journey, Janine, shall we?" He helped Janine until she finally was able to stand up. She glanced at Right Whisper for a moment, only mouthed an apology, and then placed Right Whisper comfortably in her snowsuit without losing her poise; several seconds later she gazed at the trees with a smile on her face.

"It was nice meeting you guys and thank you again for your help!" said Janine in a loud voice, hoping they heard her. "By the way, what are your names?"

"Come on, Janine, before they change their minds about us?" Corvus said, hoping they did not have to undergo the same type of traveling again.

"Why would they change their minds? They were kind enough to help us. I mean, me."

"Look at them! How tall are you compared to them? Do you want to go through the same journey again?"

"Well it wasn't so...bad. But I was thrown around a bit, wasn't I?"

"Ah huh," said Corvus with a bemused look on his face.

"Since you put it that way, we better go!" she agreed.

Janine and Corvus were about to leave when suddenly they were spoken to.

"Our names are Arbors!" puffed one of the trees in a high-pitch voice, which seemed like it was ventilating

"Nice to meet you. Thanks again. We have to run," Janine said as Corvus tugged her arm.

"Janine! Get into gear, please!" demanded Corvus.

They were getting close, but how close he was not sure. Being able to pinpoint the exact location was not going to be an easy task.

Finally, he found a sheltered area and they rested for a few minutes.

"That was quite the ride you encountered and it looks like you've met some acquaintances, but we must progress if we are to accomplish this goal. Now, I am going to fly up above and we must try again. Can you do that for me?"

Still feeling a little unstable on her feet, Janine managed to stay abreast with Corvus. Considering what she just experienced, she thought that she did pretty well to not give up on such an undertaking. Even though she took a vow to find the snow queen, she continued to feel unsure of herself. Her fear of doubt persisted, causing an uneasiness, which she felt she was unable to control.

Her negative thoughts seemed to take over until she began to cry. Whenever a new challenge turned up, she thought of the worst consequences, when she is not prepared to confront them and her emotions get the best of her. The thought of making a mistake that will cause the birds and animals to die was her main concern.

"What is the matter, Janine?" asked Right Whisper. "Why are you crying? Did you hurt yourself?"

Janine answered as she unzipped her snowsuit and held Right Whisper. "Why is it that I always feel this way? I feel that I have no one who will understand how I feel. Will it ever go away? If only I was not so shy, things would be better for me."

"Don't be so hard on yourself. Corvus and I are here if you need us. You are safe now. I realize we still have to find the snow queen, but you are not alone, and besides with what you are doing now for yourself, you will become stronger. Just have patience Janine. You'll see that you're not alone in this world!"

"Yes, I guess so," Janine said as she hugged Right Whisper before putting the ice mirror back in her snowsuit.

Deep in her thoughts with what Right Whisper had said, she had forgotten about Corvus for a few moments, until he landed next to her and asked if she was all right. Wiping her tears from her face, she said she was fine and thanked him for his concern. Corvus responded with empathy, stating that he would not be far if she could do with some cheering on, and immediately was in the air again.

As Janine watched him take flight, she spotted, once again, the shadows growing closer and closer towards her. Her heart was beating faster. She had to make a quick decision to either hide or move swiftly like Native Americans outsmarting their enemy. She could remember when her parents took her to a native reservation up north during the summer to buy trinkets as souvenirs. Janine enjoyed their music, costumes, and friendliness towards her. She even had a chance to play with the children in the reservation and learned their ways of living as hunters. Janine always had a soft heart for the natives of America, noting quite well that they were smarter than portrayed in the 1950s' movies. It was time for her to prove she was right. She chose to move swiftly and out of sight as if she were the hunter. She began to feel better when she did not feel sorry for herself.

What a jump from fear to fearless. Her attitude was beginning to change and her stride was getting stronger and stronger as she forced her way through the deep snow. That little talk with Right Whisper, and Corvus' concern, made a world of difference to her. Focusing more on Corvus, Janine concentrated hard to find the snow queen. Even the thought of supporting Corvus was a positive reinforcement for her, because she felt she was accomplishing something in such harsh conditions. And if she should die, her achievements in her heart were not left undone. Janine was feeling much better.

Then all of a sudden, without warning, she heard a loud *bang*, like a sound of a shotgun. Instinctively, Janine ran for cover behind a bush. Crouched down, she looked around, for she knew the noise was close by. She was not eager to leave her position until Corvus gave her the signal to go ahead. Waiting in silence was the most difficult time for Janine to endure because, again, the unknown was frightening. This feeling was not in her favor. It seemed forever until suddenly, Corvus swooped down at her location. Janine jumped and let out a short gasp. It took a second before she recognized that it was Corvus.

"You startled me, Corvus," Janine said.

"Sorry," Corvus said.

"Is everything all right? Do you know what happened just now?"

"Not quite sure. But I will ask you to stay put until I get back. You hear me? I don't want anything to happen to you."

Happy to hear what Corvus had to say, Janine nodded yes and promised to stay until he got back. "Be careful, Corvus. I do not like guns or the sound they give off."

"I will do my best Janine. Remember, do not move."

"Don't be too long, and be careful."

"I won't be long and I will be careful," answered Corvus, as he flew into the sky for a better view.

Janine then proceeded to unzip her snowsuit, just enough to sneak a peak at Right Whisper.

"Did you hear that loud noise, Right Whisper?"

"Did I hear it? It sounded like a bomb. I am surprised I can hear at all after that."

"What do you think happened just now?"

"I hope it isn't what I think it was. I fear that we may be in deep trouble."

"What kind of trouble?"

"We will have to wait and see."

"Does that mean our journey has just ended, Right Whisper?"

"I am not sure. I hope not, but I am not sure," answered Right Whisper, sounding rather distressed. "Do up your snowsuit, Janine, just in case Corvus needs to move on quickly. You and I will need to conserve our energy as much as possible in order to be able to help Corvus if we need to."

"Okay."

Janine obeyed her friend without delay and hoped that Right Whisper was wrong.

Corvus was not too thrilled about scouting the area to determine where the shot came from. He flew cautiously in the air and was afraid of what he was going to see in the end. After deciding that he was unsuccessful with his search, he decided to return to Janine, but suddenly he saw something moving in the branches below. Circling from up above once more, he descended slowly to take a closer look. When he got closer, he noticed some bloodstains in the snow. Cautiously, he followed the blood trail. Using his keen eyes, Corvus hunted deeper into the forest. It wasn't until he heard a soft chirp, which directed him to the spot where the injured party was located. He finally found the wounded victim.

Meanwhile, light snow was falling again and Janine was worried about Corvus, so she decided to take a short walk. She hoped that Corvus was going to return without a scratch because staying in one place made her anxious. Janine was itching to find the snow queen, but Corvus told her to stay put. But what if he needs reinforcement? What if he is injured? What if he is caught and has no way out? Thinking about Corvus' dangerous circumstances, she ignored Right Whisper's reply and made up her mind that she was in no mood to stick around, and besides, she was getting cold.

13

Walking towards the direction she believed Corvus took, Janine thought she heard a whimper in the brush. Curious, she carefully walked towards the sound. To her surprise she saw an elderly woman wearing old clothes with a shawl drawn over her head. She was sitting by a tall fir tree, sobbing. Feeling sad for this old woman, Janine cautiously walked up to her to see if she could help.

"Hello," Janine said softly, as she examined the old woman to see if she was hurt. She repeated her greeting, but did not get a response. She then decided to walk closer to the individual, thinking maybe she did not hear Janine speaking to her. As she moved closer, the old woman was shocked to see the little girl beside her. Janine jumped when the old woman screamed. Not knowing what to say next, she put her arms and hands just above her waist and gently waved her arms up and down to warn the old woman she was not in danger.

"Who are you, and how did you know I was here?" whimpered the old woman.

"I didn't know you were here. I just heard a noise and followed it. And here you were."

"Well, you scared me," replied the old woman. "I did not expect anyone to be out here in the middle of nowhere."

"I didn't mean to. I just wanted to see if you were all right. My name is Janine. What's yours, and what are you doing here in the middle of the woods?"

"Well, I am sorry, Janine, but I did not hear you. I was just leaving my home to fetch some firewood and lost my way. Now I don't know how to get back."

"I am sorry to hear that, but I don't think I can help you, since I'm not sure where I am either…"

"This happens when you get old. You tend to forget quite easily and it can be frightfully frustrating!" explained the old woman. "I…I…just do not know what to do next. I don't want to walk further into the woods and not able to…I'm afraid of getting myself…more confused. I have looked for clues, like trying to find my own footprints, but the light snow has covered them and it's hopeless."

While Janine watched the old woman try to figure out her way back, Janine felt sad for her because she lived in the middle of the woods alone and knew the old lady needed comfort. "Just a moment, let me think about this," Janine said as she sauntered towards the nearest bush, leaving the elderly woman behind. "I'll see if I can find a clue and help you find your way home. Just wait here."

It confused the old woman to hear such a comment from a little girl. She wondered why a person would have to think of a reason of whether to help someone. It was also odd to witness Janine with her back to her talking to herself as she left abruptly. Not questioning the little girl's actions, she thought that Janine might have an imaginary friend, since most children around her age do. From past experience in dealing with children, the woman was aware that when they face a calamity, they invent a friend to speak to.

A few minutes later the little girl turned around and returned to the elderly woman.

"I...I don't generally help strangers like this, but um, I have decided to see if a friend can help me also. I mean that...if that is okay with you."

The old woman gazed at Janine for a moment or two before she interrupted. "Of course. A friend out here, you say?" looking somewhat bewildered. "That would be fine. I hope your friend can come soon, because I am getting very cold out here." She was thoroughly convinced that the little girl was just imaging.

"I am sure my friend will come if I call," said Janine. "I'll call right now, okay?"

"Sure," said the old woman, going along with the game.

Janine picked a clear spot and called for Corvus several times.

"Now all we have to do is wait!" Janine said as she pointed up into the sky. "It should not take too long."

"Of course, my dear," while patting her arms and sitting on a fir log.

"I might as well tell you again what my name is..."

"It's Janine. I know, I heard you the first time," intruded the old woman. "How do you do? It is a very nice name, Janine. Is it French?"

"Yes, it is!"

"You can call me Ella," she said, extending her right hand to greet Janine. "I have lived in this part of the country for a long time. I do not like the city folk, too much hustle and bustle. I'd rather inhale the fresh air and do my own thing without being disturbed by neighbors. If your friend can find my place, then we can sit by the fire and drink a nice cup of cocoa and get warmed up. Would you like that, Janine?"

"That sounds nice."

"Good. Now we will just have to wait for your fri..."

"Corvus, you finally made it. I am so glad to see you. Is every..."

Corvus motioned Janine not to say anything more and studied the old woman sitting by the log. Instantly, he asked Janine to see him briefly, and away from the older individual.

"Why did you not stay where I told you to?" whispered Corvus.

"I was worried about you and I could not stay in one place because you may have needed my help and I was antsy," replied Janine. She was somewhat upset with Corvus' coarse attitude.

"I specifically told you to not...you just don't go wandering off like this without telling me, knowing very well that I have to go out and look for you too. You must do as you are told or else you will get lost out here. Is that understood?"

"Fine!"

"Fine!"

"Is everything all right with you two?" asked Ella.

"Yes!" the duo answered.

"Can you just wait a minute or two? I have something to discuss with Janine," requested Corvus.

"Yes...of course," answered Ella.

"Corvus," said Janine.

"What?"

"Corvus, I heard a sound out here and I found her crying. What did you expect me to do? Leave her?"

"No. Of course not, but..."

"But nothing. We need to find her home so that she does not have to freeze out here. And I sure could use some rest for a while. She promised some hot cocoa."

"Well, we will have to hurry. I will try to find her place and then we must go. Is that clear?"

"Okay! But what about hot cocoa?"

"We will see," cawed Corvus

"Is everything all right with what happened earlier?" questioned Janine.

"Ah, huh!" Corvus answered, not wanting to say too much.

It was not uncommon in the spirit world to see different walks of life, like a bird and a child, corresponding with one another, as long as they were able to communicate well. So when the two walked back to greet Ella and explained to her what their plan was, she did not seem astounded, nor demonstrated any emotion. Just a fixed stare when Corvus asked specific questions of what the home looked like and approximately how long she was out in the woods. After he received all of the particulars, he then proceeded to search until he was successful.

Returning quickly, Janine and the old woman followed his directions, and it was not long before they reached their destination.

It would seem that sitting by the fire with hot cocoa made it a pleasant stay for both Corvus and Janine, but Corvus accidently spilled the mugs close by the fireplace and warned Janine not to mention it. Shortly thereafter, the guests decided to leave while Ella was preparing a meal in the kitchen.

"Leaving already?" asked Ella.

"Yes, we have a long way to go and it is time for us to skedaddle," said Corvus.

"Yes," answered Janine. "Corvus wants me to leave right now since we only have few hours left until it gets dark. He also wants to help me find my way home and the more time we spend here the less time we have," Janine said softly. "But thank you for having us over. The cocoa was delicious, and the fire was nice."

Corvus also nodded with appreciation and was the first one out the door.

Knowing very well she had to hurry, Janine put on her snowsuit, boots, mitts, and scarf quickly and followed Corvus out the door.

"Are you sure you do not want to stay for the night?"

"Quite sure," they both answered.

Ella smiled and waved, saying, "Be careful and have a safe journey! Thank you again for your help!" Suddenly, she felt a sharp pain in her chest and immediately closed the door.

It was not long after Corvus and Janine disappeared into the forest, when Corvus explained that they had to move swiftly. Sitting by the fire was grand, but having to hurry out the door and back into the wilderness at dusk was not too thrilling for Janine. The snow had stopped falling, but darkness was beginning to surround them. She knew they would have to pick up the pace before they had to settle somewhere for shelter. Deep down, Janine felt something was bothering Corvus tremendously, but she just could not figure out what it was. Why did Corvus spill the cocoa without an explanation?

In the time being, Ella began to clean up after her company left. When she reached the living room where the cups of cocoa were sitting on the coffee table, she noticed a brown spot by the side of the chesterfield, close to the fireplace. As she got closer to the stain, she realized what it was and let out an aggravating yell.

14

Corvus and Janine heard Ella's screech and both knew they had to move immediately. Janine found out from Corvus that the chocolate milk was mixed with an herb that Faeran used to subdue his victims. Corvus had come across the herb before and the chocolate did not cover up the smell of the dissolved plant.

As they hurried through the forest, Janine had forgotten about Ella and the cocoa and made sure to concentrate on her footing. She also made sure that Right Whisper was comfortably placed in her suit.

Corvus led her into a small meadow where a boarded-up cabin was situated, surrounded by fir trees. He landed on the rooftop of the little abandoned cabin and asked Janine to help him remove the boards from the door and enter. Going along with his orders, she at last had a place to rest and feel safe for a while, never expecting to see what she witnessed when she opened the door.

Corvus almost knocked her over trying to get past her, but she stood there mesmerized by the sight of the figure in front of them. This large white bird, which appeared to be about two feet long with a dark flecking on its breast and under parts, was wounded. She did notice though that the head was pure white with a black beak but no ear tuffs. Instinctively, she wanted to check to see if there was anything she could do, but realized that it looked serious. The bird's eyes were closed, but she could see its diaphragm moving ever so slightly. The massive left wing, which drooped on one side, appeared broken, with its feathers matted with blood down to its black talons.

Janine was not sure how to approach the bird, but as she got closer, it did not make an attempt to attack nor remove itself from its location. It had blood flowing from its wing, and the injury must have been too severe for the bird to move. At least it had straw and water for survival and a roof over its head to keep it warm. That much she was thankful for. Janine noticed that it was still breathing. Shallow breathing, but breathing, and she knew that it did not have a lot of time to live.

"Corvus," whispered Janine, "who or what is this huge bird doing here? And how did it manage to find this place?"

"It's an abandoned chicken coop," answered Corvus, as he tended to the bird's wound, using the pail of snow to stop the pain and bleeding with gentle care. "Remember the big bang we heard a while ago?"

"Yes."

"Well, I finally found him lying in the bushes and he directed me to this place."

"So, who is he and what happened to him?"

"Someone used him as target practice and left him to die."

"How could someone be so cruel?" Janine mourned. "Such a beautiful bird. People are so mean." Janine petted it softly and noticed the bird's half-closed, yellow, sad eyes looking back at her.

"We must move it from this broken-down wooden floor as soon as possible, or else it will bleed to death. It needs immediate care," cawed Corvus.

"We cannot move it now. It is badly hurt. You will make it even worse. It needs a doctor!" Janine demanded.

"Do you know who this bird is? Do you have any idea?" asked Corvus. "Think, Janine!"

Janine thought for a few seconds and then with a surprised look on her face, she said, "No…it can't be?" as she looked at Corvus with amazement.

Corvus nodded his head with acknowledgement. "Yes it is! The big kahuna! The snow queen's guardian. She is the only one who can save him. That is why we have to leave now!"

"How did we ever…I mean, how were we so lucky to find him? Not like this, but I mean like he fell right under our noses. We didn't have to look for him hard. Did we…I mean, you found him, Corvus. You are the hero. You! But, are you sure this is the right guardian for the snow queen?"

"Yes, he is the right one. He told me so," Corvus said.

"He actually spoke to you? Yet, he is hardly moving and he looks pretty bad."

"That is why we have to save him soon, like right now!" Corvus said excitedly. "We mustn't forget the snow queen as well. You need to remove your scarf and give it to me. Now quickly, get the sled out back!"

"But I don't understand you, Corvus. He will die if we move him, won't he?" Janine cried. "He has to get well first before…"

"Janine, trust me on this one. He needs to be on his own grounds, not here," Corvus said as he headed towards the door to open it for Janine.

Janine threw her scarf at Corvus and ran out of the chicken coop and found the sled. She had doubts about the owl's survival. Sliding the sled into the chicken coop was not so difficult as she thought, but putting a bird with a broken wing and a gunshot wound on the sled without hurting it was going to be a chore. It was something she was not looking forward to doing.

She found some more straw lying about in the building nearby to use as a cushion. She then placed the wounded owl on the small sleigh, with Corvus' help, ever so gently, but just as she had predicted earlier, the owl screamed. Apologizing immediately, she continued to put more straw around the bird to keep him warm and comfortable. At the same time Corvus used Janine's scarf as a sling for the owl's broken wing. While Janine was trying to pull and push the sleigh out of the coop, the door did not stay open. She finally found a piece of wood outside to hold the door open, so it would not slam on her face. She was going to ask Corvus for help, but he was too busy cleaning up the mess in the coop, so she decided to do this herself, feeling somewhat neglected by Corvus, which was not his style. Just as she was heading out the door, he told Janine he would join her as soon as possible, once he was finished with what he had to do. She proceeded to carefully maneuver the sleigh out of the coop as Corvus covered the bird entirely with straw.

15

Finally, with a lot of huffing and puffing, she was pulling the sleigh out into the meadow, through fresh snow, which made it easy to maneuver. But which way was she to go? Where was Corvus to direct them? This was not like him. Did he not tell her he would join her soon?

But there was no sign of him anywhere. She called him several times, but no response. She ran back to the coop, but found no sight of Corvus. She returned to the sleigh and called, but still no answer. Her heart began to beat faster, since she was worried about saving the bird's life and her own safety. How will she ever be able to get help out here, given that she did not know what direction to take to find the snow queen?

Janine stopped pulling the sled to have a word with Right Whisper. No sooner did she think of her troubled situation, she felt something closing in on her. She knew it was not Corvus because the approach was different. The feeling she had was eerie and she could not shake if off. Without warning, there he was, standing in front of her.

Faeran!

The grotesque phantom and his two guards were staring right at her as she gradually zipped up her snowsuit. With her heart pounding, knowing very well that she had to make a decision as to how to escape from his magic, she had to come up with a plan. Her fear of failing transpired again.

"Well, well, well. We meet again. Look at her boys, a scared-dee cat, right in front of us!" Faeran and his sidekicks laughed her.

"I'm not," Janine answered, in a broken voice as she tried to contain her fear.

"What are you doing out here in the middle of a meadow? And where are you going with that?" as he pointed to the sleigh. "Going for a stroll, Janine? Or are you meeting someone? I don't see anyone around here. Where are your friends? Did they leave without you? That is, if you have any friends. I don't see them around to protect or help you," mocked Faeran. "I think she is all, alone, boys. With no one to rescue her."

Noticing that Faeran's guards were also beginning to encircle her, Janine decided to stay in front of the sleigh, holding onto the rope and hoping that Corvus would come real soon.

"Stay away from me!" bellowed Janine as she observed her enemies. "I said, stay away or I'll..."

"Or what? Do you think that we are going to listen to you? You have already gone too far with this escapade and I am not about to let you get away with it again, little girl. You are not going to outwit my powers for a stupid owl and the snow queen. Besides, you are mine now, Janine. One day Corvus will be mine too, once he loses his confidence, and I will subdue him and have him surrender to my way of thinking. Just like my boys here. You have no guts to overcome your fear, which makes me a more powerful force against your soul," the phantom said as he displayed his strong white glow that encased him.

Janine started to cry and said, "How did you know about my mission and...and Corvus?"

"Ah, look boys, she's crying," smiled Faeran. "It's my business to know. Now, enough with the chit-chat. Give me the sleigh, Janine."

"No!"

"No, you say? Then I guess my guards will have to take it away from you."

"I am taking this sleigh and I am going to locate the snow queen, and to hell with you and your goons. You are not going to touch me or this precious bird either or else..." Janine muttered as she was trying to compose herself and protect the sleigh.

"Really?" Faeran said. "How interesting! I find your story quite amusing, trying to save a dumb bird that is half dead. Fascinating!"

"It's true!" Janine stammered.

"Stop! You are only lying to yourself, Janine. You are not going anywhere and this bird will not see the snow queen now, or ever. Is that clear? Do you know that being courageous can get you into a lot of trouble? Especially when you do not know where to go and you are only fooling yourself," Faeran explained, as he grabbed Janine by the edge of her suit and dragged her away from the injured bird.

"Let me go!" yelled Janine, trying to release herself from Faeran's grip.

"You know what to do boys!" Faeran hollered.

The guards grabbed the sleigh and pulled the rope from her hand. To her mortification, she visualized a horrible ordeal. Trying to escape from the phantom, she saw the guards spearing into the straw. Janine could not help the victim. Screaming and crying, she yelled at them to stop, but she was powerless in saving the bird. Now, she was without hope. How was she going to explain this to Corvus? She gave up trying to break away from Faeran. Janine slumped onto the ground like a rag doll. She had lost her energy and hope. Faeran had won once again. She was going to be his prisoner. She did not care anymore. They had taken away a precious soul and she was unable to save it.

"Time to leave, Janine. You are mine now for all eternity," said Faeran. "Don't look so gloomy, girl. I will take good care of you. Come boys. We are finished here. There is much to celebrate, now that I have gained more power!" Faeran laughed.

The two guards followed their orders immediately and started to approach Faeran, when suddenly they were swept off their feet. Yelling from fright, they noticed that they were high off the ground, held by branches they have never seen before.

Screaming for mercy, they asked Faeran to help them. Faeran, too, was not sure what was going on since he was feeling excruciating chest pain, unexpectedly, and tried to apprehend Janine by force, but recognized that he had to move quickly to avoid losing his powers over her.

Janine slowly looked up and immediately knew who they were and smiled at the sight of the Arbors.

As the phantom was about to leave, he did not anticipate what was in store for him next. Little people were beginning to appear. They were coming in great numbers, to the point that he was losing his powers and gaining more sharp pains rather rapidly. Janine could feel that his hold was not as strong as it was and started to wiggle away from his grip. Examining their faces carefully, Janine was sure that she saw these little people before, but where? Then she knew. But how was it possible that they were not ordinary children? How did they escape from that horrible place? Then, all of a sudden, each of the children began to grow to their normal sizes.

The glow from Faeran's strength began to disappear. His power was fading away and he knew that if this would continue, the pain would be unbearable. He then decided to let Janine go and make haste or else he would vanish forever.

He quickly turned to Janine and said in a stern tone, "I will not forget you. One day, without warning, I will return and you will be mine. But for now, I will bid you adieu!"

With great difficulty, Faeran finally evaporated, leaving his guards behind.

Janine was happy and sad at the same time and was thankful that the Arbors came to her rescue. But it was too late to save the snowy owl.

16

Facing the Arbors who held Faeran's guards, Janine motioned the branches to bring the guards closer to her. As they were in front of her, she glared at their faces, and said very slowly, "I despise you. You have no feelings for anyone else but your selfish souls. There are no words to describe what you did to that poor defenseless bird out there, but I can assure you that you will be severely punished for what you did. I hope that I will never have to see your faces again. You are nasty and dangerous and you need to be put away forever. These Arbors, I am sure, will find such a place for you two!"

"I hate you!" yelled one of the guards as they tried to break away, but failed.

"For now, but maybe one day, you will realize the mistakes you have made!" Janine snapped.

"What do you want us to do with them now, Janine?" questioned one of the Arbors.

"Hold on to them for a while, so that I may think of what to do next, but right now I must bury the snowy owl," Janine said sadly.

"You have no right to keep us here!" screeched one of the guards.

The children followed Janine as she approached the sleigh and hesitated. She was not eager to see the owl's demise. Before she was about to remove the straw, she asked them one question. "How did you become children again, since you were prisoners in the cave?"

She waited for a few seconds before one of them answered, "You are right, we were prisoners from the phantom's hold for a long time. Just like you, we were victims of fear and ignorance. As immigrants with a language barrier, our parents and friends were our judges. We, as children, did not have much of a say. They took care of all the decision-making. Therefore, in time, we became afraid of questioning and failing in front of everyone. Consequently, we became ignorant and afraid to express our feelings for fear of being made fun of if we made a mistake."

"Oh," murmured Janine, as she reviewed their faces.

Then one of the children blurted out, "But then when we found your parcel, and saw the walnuts, we were curious, so we ate them. Like magic, we began to feel different. We were not afraid anymore and it was then we heard that you were in trouble with Faeran. The Arbors also wanted to help you, so they helped us find you here."

"I am glad you found me and thank you. I know what you are talking about." Janine nodded her head, knowing very well in her heart she had a long ways to go to overcome her fears.

As she was about to remove the straw from the sleigh, the children placed their little hands over their faces to avoid the view. She also thought that she heard her name being called from a nearby bush, but ignored it. As she removed the straw from the sleigh, everyone and everything went silent.

Janine was astounded from what she saw. She quickly began to remove all of the straw from the sleigh and look underneath it as well. Dumbfounded by the whole thing.

"Where is it? What do we do next?" asked one of the children.

" I do not know. How will I ever explain this one to Corvus? He is not going to be happy with me," Janine said as she sat down beside the sled. "Where is the guardian?"

"Right here! Are you deaf? Janine! Did you not hear me calling your name?" grumbled Corvus as he rushed out of the bushes, waddling towards her.

Janine sprang up onto her feet. "Where were you?"

"For your information, I was hiding behind those bushes," Corvus said gruffly as he pointed to the direction of his stay. "And I did call you several times, but you ignored me! Why? Why did you do that? Why not follow your instincts?"

"I...I...I had to take care...I mean, I thought I had to bury the snowy owl. Oh, it is my entire fault. I lost the snowy owl. I don't know where he is and he could be dead by now. I am so sorry, Corvus." It was then Janine began to cry, sobbing uncontrollably.

Right Whisper felt sorry for Janine, but knew that she had to find a way to release her own grief. The children went to her immediately and wrapped their arms around her to ease the pain.

Noticing the sincerity of the whole ordeal, Corvus let it go, for he too felt her grief, and said, "I am sorry for unsettling you, but I had to remove the owl immediately from the sled. You see, I had a feeling danger was approaching and I could not risk losing this precious owl and replaced him with some old burlap bag lying on the coop floor," explained Corvus. "I needed you to be sincere, to outsmart Faeran. And making him think that they had killed the snowy owl would avoid any suspicion. I am sorry that I had to put you through this, but the plan would not have worked if Faeran knew there was doubt in your heart."

"I suppose you had to do what was best, Corvus, but we must get this owl to the snow queen at once," said Janine.

Without wasting time, Corvus ran back to where the owl was lying and checked for any signs of life. The others followed immediately.

"We can't waste any time, Snow Scandiaca. Tell me where the snow queen is?" whispered Corvus to the owl.

"The circle of the trees," murmured the owl and then fainted.

"I know where that is, but I have to hurry," Corvus said to himself.

Since watching the owl's suffering was not a pleasant sight, a decision had to be made immediately. The Arbors were chosen by Corvus to help reach the destination on time because of the terrain they covered in such a short time.

The owl was carefully placed on one of the Arbor's branches, which was cupped like a nest, and Janine was swiftly picked up to hold him in position so that he would not fall out of the tree. Janine knew deep down in her soul that the only person who could save the owl was the snow queen and that there was no time to waste. The owl's breathing was quite shallow and Janine had doubts that it would survive this journey. At this point, it seemed like a miracle was their only chance.

The children also rode on the Arbors, and Corvus led the way. The question now was: will Corvus be able to find the exact location where the snow queen resided or get lost in the process?

"Where are we going, Corvus?" shouted Janine. "Is it close by?"

"It's not far! We should reach the circle of trees shortly. Keep your eyes peeled. We need all the help we can get."

"The what trees?"

"The circle of trees! It can only be found when the sky is clear, and when you are flying up above, you are able to see a circle of trees. They are actually willow trees growing in the swamp, but the only difference is that these trees grow in a circle, which protects the snow queen. No one can enter or exit except the snowy owl. He is the only one who is her pair of eyes outside the circle if there is need to balance the winter season."

"What makes you think that she will let you in the circle?" Janine questioned.

"I don't, but I will surely try. Anyway, she is asleep. How will she know that I have arrived or invaded her sacred ground?"

"You are probably right? How will she save the owl?" said Janine while she heard Right Whisper mumbling in her snowsuit.

"Just a minute, Right Whisper," Janine said, as she managed to unzip her snowsuit. "I did not hear what you said."

"Do not lose faith, Janine. Keep going regardless. Sometimes things may look bad, but things change for the better," Right Whisper explained.

"I hope that you are right. We have to have a positive outlook on things even though it looks bad, don't we?" Janine questioned Right Whisper.

"Let's wait and see, shall we? Let's keep our fingers crossed," said Right Whisper. Janine nodded and left her snowsuit opened.

The Arbors walked as fast as they could to keep up with Corvus, and Janine tried to make the owl as comfortable as she could with all the moving around. Finally, Corvus shouted that he saw the circle of trees. Janine and the children began to cheer with delight.

"We made it, Janine," said Right Whisper. "Your mission is almost over, and soon you will be able to rest from all of this. You should be proud of yourself, for this is quite an accomplishment!"

"Ya," stated Janine with sadness in her heart, for she knew that her stay would be limited and that she needed to hold on as much as she could to be with them. "Ya, I will miss you all."

As soon as the Arbors stood in front of the willow trees, one of willows bellowed. "Stop! Do not step any further! You are trespassing! No one is allowed in these grounds! Turn around immediately and go back where you came from if you do not wish to be harmed." The willow tree swirled its long thin branches towards them.

"Hurt? Did I hear you right? You would hurt innocent children? How dare you speak to us that way? Children love playing in the woods and you have the nerve to threaten us? Who is your leader? I wish to speak to the person-in-charge," Janine said sternly. She was not in the mood to argue or be pushed around again. She had had enough and knew that no time was to be wasted to save the owl.

Noticing that Janine was furious and not backing down, they asked her what was her purpose in being there.

"I have the snow queen's guardian and he is badly hurt. Can you help us?" she asked calmly, while Corvus landed on one of the Arbor's branches nearby.

"How do you know it is the snow queen's protector and not a trick?"

"Are you calling me a liar? Come and see for yourself," as she pointed to the nest where he laid in her arms. "You must hurry; he is dying."

"I'm sorry, we cannot help you, little girl. You must run along and try to save the bird some other way because the snow queen's protector never gets caught or hurt. It is a brave and a perfect bird. You must be mistaken. This is another bird!" said one of the willow trees, ignoring Janine's plea.

"Oh, really?" yelled Janine. "Well, I guess I will have to shout my way into your circle to wake up the queen! Arbors, please put me down."

The Arbors instantly obeyed and she was placed on the ground gently. "Thank you! See I remembered what you said earlier."

Janine decided to make her way through the willow trees carrying the owl in her arms and began to try and find the snow queen when Corvus interrupted her.

"Shh," said Corvus, "you are embarrassing us. Maybe we can find another diplomatic way of seeing the queen. How about it, Janine? Are you listening to me? Janine, Janine, where are you going? Why are you walking away from me when I am talking to you? Janine, I don't like where this is going?"

"Trust me! Remember how you told me to trust you once or twice. Now it is my turn. Right Whisper? Right Whisper, are you there?"

"I am right here. Go for it. You have nothing to lose," replied Right Whisper.

"Thanks, Right Whisper. I knew I could count on you, and no, I have nothing to lose."

"All right, you big oafs!" hollered Janine to the willows. "I want to speak to the queen at once, or I will leave the guardian at your trunks and the bird will be your responsibility. And if it dies and the queen sees this, she will probably have you cut down."

"You would not dare," said one of the willow trees.

"Try me."

"Yeah! Try her," said Corvus.

"We double-dare you!" the children hollered simultaneously to the willows.

For a brief moment there was silence, and when Janine was about to charge, the willow trees spoke briefly to each other and then decided to make way for her to cross the meadow ahead. A bright light shone in front of her and motioned Janine to follow it.

Everyone was in awe except for the willow trees. Janine was blinded by the light and preceded to walk slowly, covering her eyes as she carried the owl carefully with Corvus following behind. She thanked the trees for not stopping her.

Once her eyes got used to the light, she came across a large hollow tree covered with colorful feathers, and noticed there was a body lying quite still in it. She could not take her eyes off of how lovely the queen was.

The snow queen looked so beautiful with her long wavy black hair down to her waist. She wore a gold band across her soft, fair-skinned forehead, a long white robe, and white mukluks on her feet. She looked so peaceful. Janine felt like she was floating towards the hollow of the tree where the queen stayed and was anxious as to what may come. Instantly, Janine stood by the snow queen and proceeded to speak.

"Excuse me, your Royal Highness. I have come a long way and you need to listen to me right away. You need to wake up and save the guardian and all of the birds and animals immediately or else they will die."

Everyone was silent.

"Please wake up. You are their only hope. How can you ignore them?"

The children, Corvus, and the Arbors stood close to Janine, hoping the queen heard their plea once again. They waited for a minute or two, but there was no response. Then Janine decided to check on the snowy owl to see if there was any change in his condition just in case the queen used her magic powers to save his life, but when she examined it, the snowy owl was already dead.

With tears in her eyes, Janine laid the protector beside the queen and covered him with part of the queen's long, shiny robe.

While Janine petted the bird and then moved her head to look at the beautiful snow queen, a tear accidentally fell on the queen, for in her heart she knew she did the best she could to save the snowy owl, the animals, and the birds. Everyone began to follow her out of the meadow when she heard a soft voice speak to her.

"Janine," (small cough) "Janine, don't go just yet. It takes a lot of courage to force you to see me. You are a brave little girl. I want to thank you for saving my precious protector and I will never forget your bravery, nor forget all the others who were involved. Thank you to you all!"

Janine and the others turned slowly to where the voice came from and, to their surprise, there stood the beautiful snow queen facing them with the snowy owl on her arm.

"I was waiting for Snow Scandiaca to arrive, but his journey took longer than it should have. So I rested and lost track of time. Now, I will grant you your wish, and you will enjoy the birds and animals this year, and the year after, and so on. You have done so much for me that it is time for you to go home and be with your family now, Janine."

Janine could not believe what she heard and was so overwhelmed and happy that something went right and that the others were content too. She will finally go home and be with her parents and sister. It was a long journey and time to go home. She ran towards the snow queen, gave her a big hug, and said, "Thank you." She knew all would be well and back to normal. However, she knew that she would miss her present friends and Corvus. With tears in her eyes she looked at them all and hoped that their friendship would not come to an end. She took Right Whisper out of her snowsuit, kissed the mirror, and said, "Thank you for all you have done for me. I am so glad we had met and that you had faith in me."

"You will not be forgotten, Janine."
It was then Janine suddenly felt very tired and wanted to find a soft, warm, dry place to sleep.

"If you do not mind, I am feeling rather tired and I would like to find a place to rest. Can you help me, snow queen?"

"Why, of course! You had a long trip and a great deal of strife to deal with. Please follow me and I will make you as comfortable as possible," said the snow queen tenderly.

"It has been long journey. Corvus, don't leave me when I wake up. Promise me. I want to thank all of you for helping me," Janine pointed out. "I...I...think I found the place. Just let me lie down for a while. Right Whisper, maybe Corvus can take us back later? Don't leave me," yawned Janine as she found a cozy space to sleep. Even though Janine was quite tired, she could not believe how lovely her area in which to sleep was.

The queen led her into a small ground fort covered with twigs and snow, but inside was different than what she had expected it to be. The ground floor was plastered with long green leaves similar to the willow trees leaves, at about three inches thick, and then coated with the colored feathers on top, identical to the snow queen's bed. All the inside walls were covered with white sparkles. What a delightful sight when she sat comfortably on the cushiony green leaves.

"No, Corvus will not do that. It will be I who will return you back safely," said the snow queen. "It is the least I can do for you since you saved our lives. Sweet dreams, Janine."

"Corvus, Corvus, do not leave me. I love you Corvus," Janine whispered as she drifted away to sleep.

"I won't, and I love you, too," whispered Corvus. "Remember something for me, will you?"

"What?" asked Janine, sleepily.

"I will become your spirit."

"My spirit?"

"Yes, whenever you are emotionally upset and need spiritual guidance, I will be around. If I am perched on your right side, it is a sign that you will have the intelligence of thinking things through and if I am perched on your left side, your heart will be sensitive to the needs of others and yourself."

"How will I know this?"

"You will know. It is something that is built inside you. Because you are quite sensitive to the needs of others, you will carry a special gift. Have confidence in yourself and all will be well. It will take time and one day you will understand what I am telling you."

"Sleep, my child. Sleep," murmured the snow queen, as she and the others all gathered around, inside and outside the fort.

Again, she called out Corvus' name, but this time Janine heard a faint noise close by calling her name. Suddenly, she saw them and was not worried anymore.

"Maman, Papa, Elisabeth, you found me!" cried Janine, as she greeted her parents and sister in the woods.

"Janine, are you all right?" cried her mother.

"Yes, I am fine, but my head still hurts a bit. I fell on that tree" (as she pointed to it nearby) "and hit my head."

Her family gave her lots of hugs and, immediately, her papa picked her up, placed her on the sled they used on the icy hill, and preceded to head home. Her maman laid a warm blanket on her to keep her warm. What an affectionate welcoming she received, and she was looking forward to getting some rest.

Just as her family was ready to leave, near the icy hill, she noticed a crow perched on a nearby tree at her left side, gazing at her for only a short while. She did remember what Corvus said, and will be sensitive to others' needs and not be selfish when it was necessary to go home in the first place. She looked at the crow until it flew away, and she said to her sister, "Sorry, Elisabeth, I should have gone home with you when you were complaining of being cold," and held her sister's hand all the way home.

THE END...for now

Joëlle Hübner-McLean

About the Author

JOËLLE HÜBNER-MCLEAN was born in Nancy, France and landed as an immigrant with her parents and sister at Pier 21 Nova Scotia, Canada in the 50's and now lives in Oshawa/Perth, Ontario. Once achieving an honors degree in Bachelor of Art's in Cultural/Native Studies at Trent University in 2002 in Peterborough, Ontario and her Bachelor of Education from York University, Toronto, Ontario in 2003, with additional qualifications as a Special Education Specialist in 2007, she teaches Secondary level full time. Being interested in Native Studies and nature itself, she began writing her first novel, Corvus and Me for children ages 8 to grade 9. In addition, she had written a journal on Inuit Culture and the Genealogy of Peter Leon, which was published in Labrador and St. Augustine, Quebec. It is also under the Wild Violet Magazine (Birthday Blue) website.